FINDING CHARLEY

(FULL CIRCLE #2)

By Casey Peeler

Acknowledgements:

Special thanks to:

My husband, Billy, and daughter, Carlee, thank you for being there on this adventure. It's crazy how a year can change our lives. 2013 was a year of firsts, some good and others not the best, but change is good. I can't wait to see what 2014 has in store for us! I love you both with my whole heart!

My sister, Pam Baldwin, at Paperclutch for the cover design. You have always been there at any given moment. Cover one was an adventure for both of us, but cover two was a breeze! It is as fabulous as you! Love you!

My parents, Mike and Cindy, thanks for believing in me like you always do! Parental support is important no matter your age!

Chelly Peeler, you've had my back from day one. You have helped keep up with reviews at Hardcover Therapy while I finished writing, read *NTB & FC*, read it again, edited, and given advice. We aren't just family; you truly are one of my best friends, and I couldn't have done this without you.

My betas, Paige, Tabby, Pam, and Kristina, thank you so much for your thoughts and feelings that have brought this book to life. I owe y'all!

Paige, you have read, edited, read, edited, read, and edited! I couldn't have done this without you! Round two has been amazing! I can't wait to continue our editing journey!

Southern Charms, my street team, y'all are sweet as sugar! I honestly wouldn't be where I am today without you! With each like, share, comment, and review, you've gone above and beyond each and every day! I <3 y'all!

Cortlan Allen, my cover model, now they see both sides of you! LOL :)

Brian Harris at Firelight Photography for the cover photos

My family, friends, authors, and bloggers, thanks for your thoughts, posts, shares, tweets, and likes!

For my sister, Pam. Thanks for always being my best friend since the day you entered my life, always having my back, and sticking with me through thick and thin! I love you!

Table of Contents

Previously in *No Turning Back*

We hang up and I finish putting the final touches on my makeup. As I add a little more highlight to my eye shadow, there is a knock at my door. "Hold on a sec!" I yell. I finish my left eye and walk to the door with the brush in my hand. I open the door to see Joe sitting on the floor across the hall holding an empty fifth of Jack Daniels. He pulls his piercing eyes toward mine, and I'm not sure what is going on in there, but something is beyond wrong. He staggers as he stands. He walks toward me, and if I didn't know better, I would say he is about to cry.

"Joe, you're scaring me. What's wrong? Is it your grandma?" He shakes his head no. He looks like he is trying to talk, and I'm unsure if he doesn't want to or if the news is that bad.

As he reaches my doorway, he takes his hand and embraces my cheek. "I'm so sorry, Squirrel! I'm so, so sorry." He begins to sob. I pull him close, wrap my arms around him and try to comfort him. I have no idea what is wrong, but I will help him fix it.

"Joe, what are you sorry for?" I take his face in my hands, and he looks into my eyes. He says the words I never thought I'd hear.

"It was me, Squirrel."

My mind is completely confused. What the hell is he talking about? Oh. My. God. Please tell me it isn't so. There is no way. It can't be. I take a step back without moving my eyes from him.

"What do you mean, it was you?" I can feel my heartbeat beginning to increase and my chest beginning to move double time.

"I'm so sorry. I... I... helped Dylan." I stop and replay the words over and over in my head. Then it hits me like a Mack truck. I start to shake my head no as tears fall down my face. This cannot be happening. He nods his head yes, and this is all the reassurance I need before I lose my damn mind.

The heat begins to rise to my face. My insides begin to tremble, and I use every ounce of my being to fight back. "Get out!" I grit through my teeth. "GET OUT! I said!" He continues to stand there. My voice crescendos to a screeching yell. I make my way toward him as I say the words one more time with an added choice word. "Get the FUCK out now!" I walk up to him and try to push him out of my room. He doesn't budge. I begin to scratch, punch, spit, and use words that I never knew were in my vocabulary as tears continue to stream down my face. "G-g-g-get out!" I cry.

An audience has begun to build around my doorway. Joe attempts to move from my room, but not before I realize someone else is removing him. Tori, Anna, Jenny, Cassie, Caroline, and Georgia are trying their damnedest to move him. Tori is at a loss for words, which I have never seen. The world is revolving around me, but I am completely still.

Joe is in the hallway, and I hear Georgia. "Joe, I think it's time you left. I don't know what the hell's going on, but you will not hurt her. Do you hear me?" She is talking like she is my mother. "If I hear one word about Dylan Sloan, you or anyone else involved, I will hunt you down and whoop your ass myself. Got it?!" Tori's face is puzzled with the mention of Dylan's name. "Get the hell out of here before I call campus police." Joe does not talk. He takes his fifth and stumbles down the hall. The girls are completely shocked, and Georgia rushes to my side.

Mascara runs down my face. I fall to the floor, and every ounce of fight I have is long gone. Georgia embraces me, and a dark, deep sob escapes my chest that I have been holding back for seventeen months. Georgia reaches across to my bed, picks up my phone and scrolls through my contacts. She finds the only one that has ever mattered and hits *Send*.

"Char-coal, what's goin' on?"

"Cash, this is Georgia." There is a long pause. "Joe is helping Dylan."

Chapter 1

Silence. Complete silence.

"Cash, did you hear me?" Georgia states cautiously.
Silence.

"Georgia, what do you mean, it was Joe?" Cash grits
through his teeth.

Georgia takes a deep breath. Inhale. Exhale. She
chooses her words carefully. "We were getting ready to go
to Whiskey River, and Joe showed up here tonight. He was
drunk and crying. He just kept saying he was sorry, but we
didn't know what for. Then, he just blurted it out."

"Georgia, I'm heading to the truck now. Don't leave
her alone. I'll be there as fast as the F250 can go."

Georgia has a complete change in demeanor as she
looks at me. I begin to shake harder as waves of countless
emotions pass through me. I want Cash. I need Cash, but
Georgia thinks otherwise because I can see it in her eyes.

"Um, Cash, I think you need to stay in Grassy Pond."
As Georgia speaks, I completely stop. My tears and sobs
extinguish. The only thing that remains is the trembling
from my head to my toes, but I'm fully pulled out of my
meltdown. I knew she wanted to tell Cash to stay home,
but to actually go through with it is a different story. No
one has ever told Cash no when it comes to me. I can hear
him through the phone, and I know it's a cluster of four-
letter words. He's not going to listen to her. Georgia is
trying to get in a word, but all she manages are parts of
syllables. Finally, she takes a breath and makes him stop in
his tracks.

"Hear me out, Cash. I'm here, and you're there. Don't take this the wrong way, but you can't always be here to rescue her. Let the girls and me see if we can help things. If in a few hours it's not going okay, then you can come. All right?"

Oh hell, what is he thinking? I know he isn't going to just wait in Grassy Pond. I listen as he begins to speak loudly enough that the speakerphone isn't needed.

"I can't do that! I can't just let someone hurt her again. If I don't come to help Charley, at least I can beat Joe's ass. Something… I've got to do something!"

"Exactly, Cash, you can let her do this alone. Isn't that what she's been wanting? Here's your chance to show her how much you really love her. I promise either I will call or she will in two hours."

"Can I at least talk to her?"

Georgia takes the phone and hands it to me.

"Char-coal, will you talk to me?" I hear the truck crank.

"You're on your way?" I question. Georgia darts her eyes at me.

"I was already in the truck by the time Georgia and I finished our conversation. I haven't left the farm. What do you want me to do?"

As I wipe the tears and mascara from my eyes, I take a minute and realize that Georgia is right. This is my opportunity to do this without a guy in my life. Here goes nothing!

"Cash Money, as much as I want you here with me, this is my chance to make it on my own. I'm not sure that I can, but Georgia's here. I only have to make it through exams, and then I'll be home."

I hear Cash take a deep breath before saying the words I never thought would come out of his mouth.

"Only 'cause you asked, Char-coal. I'll stay here until you need me, and then I'll be there fast as lightnin'. I do have a question for ya. Do you want me to tell Tessa?"

My heart stops, and my hands begin to shake. No, Tessa can't know. Tessa knows just what she needs to know. She will worry herself sick if she knows all this mess with Dylan is still going on, and she only knows half of it.

"Please don't tell Tessa. Cash, promise me you won't call her," I barely say as I start to sob again. I attempt to pull it together or he will change his mind for sure.

"Are you sure you're okay without me?" Cash questions.

"No, but let me try. I promise I'll call you in a little while. I love you, Cash Money."

"I love you, too, Char-coal. Now, promise me you'll call."

"I will." We disconnect the line, and it's one of the hardest things I have ever done. It's like my heart is breaking all over again, just like when I drove away from the club that December night. There is one difference though. This time I know that it's for the right reasons, even if I don't think I'm strong enough.

After taking the phone from my hands, Georgia places it on the floor and sits next to me. She pulls me in to her little short self, and I fall apart completely. She wraps her arms around me and doesn't let go. The tears continue to fall, and she holds me for what feels like hours. We don't talk; we just sit. Georgia is the friend that I have always needed in my life. I know now why God changed my plans this summer. He knew that I needed friends outside of Grassy Pond, and Georgia is at the top of this list. As my breathing begins to level, there's a knock at the door. It's Tori.

"Um, Charley, I don't know what that was about, but I'm here for ya. We aren't going tonight. You need us more than a night at a bar." I shake my head no.

"Y'all go on. There's no need to join this pity party. I've been here before."

Tori looks at Georgia, shrugs her shoulders and leaves the room. Well, damn, I didn't think she'd bail that fast! Before I have time to realize what is going on, the girls of Kluft are in my room dressed like they are ready for a night out on the town, but instead of booze, they have sodas and pretzel sticks.

Everyone piles on my floor, and we sit in silence. They need to know what's going on, but I don't know if I can tell them or if I even want to.

The tension within these four walls is thick. Before I talk, Tori puts some pretzels into her mouth and acts like they are walrus teeth. I can't help but smile when she begins to speak. Then, all the other Kluft girls do the same as they start to rap "Gin & Juice". I'm not better, but I now know that I have friends that I can count on at

Southern. There's just one problem. They don't know the entire truth, and I'm not sure if I'm ready to spill it yet.

When their rap session ends, I realize I have to say something. But what?

"Thanks, but y'all really don't have to do that. Y'all could have gone out. I'll be alright."

They shake their head in unison, and I know there is no way they are going anywhere.

Caroline is the first to respond, and when she does, it speaks volumes. "Charley, girl, I don't know what the hell that was all about, but I know one thing. You're one of us, and we aren't going to let you go through this alone. I'm ready to break a nail if needed." She slides next to me on the floor.

I pull my knees back into my chest and half grin. *Break a nail?* That's some serious shit! I take a deep breath, close my eyes, and let the words flow from my mouth. "There's a lot that I need to say, but I'm not sure I can do it or want to. The one thing I want y'all to know upfront is that I never wanted anyone to know about this, but now I have no choice."

Georgia chimes in. "Char, you don't have to say anything you don't want to. Just know we are here for you when you decide to talk. Talking is going to help fix this. Well… and time."

Everyone looks around and then back to Georgia. They know she knows.

"I know, Georgia, but I need to tell them some of it. I can't leave y'all in the dark any longer." Here goes nothing. The thought of what I'm about to relive and the name I'm about to say make me want to vomit. I take several slow, deep breaths then begin to share the most personal bit of information about me to more people than I ever wanted to know. The last time I trusted someone with these words, my life crumbled to pieces in the hallway on the other side of this door. It's hard to believe that was only a few hours ago, and here I am about to put it out there again…Dylan, that night, and the underlying current that continues to rise while I'm at Southern.

"Dylan Sloan is my ex, and let's just say it's not a fairy-tale ending. It broke me. I can't explain right now, but I will tell y'all that since I've got to school, he's been keeping tabs on me. Cash and I have been totally creeped out. Joe and Georgia knew, but I wanted to keep it to myself." I take a pause, and Caroline starts to ask a question. I put my hand up to tell her to hold on. "I've gotten crazy mail, pictures, and videos of Joe in the mountains. Joe has received crazy Facebook messages, but it all comes down to the fact the one person I trusted the most was behind it. Joe was Dylan's eyes at Southern. He's on his team and not mine."

"Oh hell, no! I'm about to go give him a piece of my mind right now! Who's with me?" Tori says as she gets up and pulls her hands into clenched fists.

I shake my head no because that is not what I want. It's not a war. It's my life, and it's time I step up to the plate and take charge.

Tori stops and looks at me like I've totally lost it, but then she takes a seat.

We all sit there quietly for a few minutes. I know this has to be a complete shock to them, but honestly, I'm surprised that Tori hasn't put things together since she's the "Queen of Google".

Georgia speaks, "Girls, I think we need to just be here until Charley decides what she wants to do. By being here, I mean, support anytime it's needed… no matter what. We are a family, and it's our job to help pick up someone when they are down. Y'all with me?"

They all shake their head and move closer to me. They huddle around me and just hold me tight until the tears begin to fall. They don't fall because I'm breaking. They fall because I'm healing. Dylan took so much from my life, but what he doesn't know is that each piece he has broken is slowly being put back together, thanks to a sisterhood I now have with the girls of Kluft.

I feel a glimpse of hope, and that grows even more when Caroline begins to pray aloud.

"Dear Lord, please put your arms around Charley. Hold her close, grant her the strength to get through this, and allow us to be there for her no matter what each of us is facing. Amen."

This warms my soul and makes me smile. Faith has always been a part of my life. Heck, there's a church on every corner in the South. Even though we are living life by doing things our parents would probably kill us if they knew about, when it comes down to it, we are ground in our roots.

As we all hold each other in a tight embrace, Hayden decides to lighten the mood. "I don't know about you guys, but I think we need another beer! Whew! That's some emotional shit we just went through!" Tori looks at her like she's not serious, and I giggle like a person in the psych ward. Everyone else follows behind me.

After our giggle session ends, the girls ask if I'm up for a movie. I'm not really sure if I am, but what the heck.

"As long as it's *Sweet Home Alabama*." With that statement, I know what I need to do. "Um, but can I call Cash first? It might be a while, but if y'all are still game afterwards, I'm in."

"You got it, Charley. We'll leave and get comfortable. Just let us know when you're ready, okay?" Caroline states.

They leave the room. Georgia stands at the door, and I give her a nod to let her know it's all right. I need a little space.

I walk to the dresser and look into the mirror. I look like I've been an extra in a horror movie. I grab a makeup-removing wipe and clean myself up before I call my Cash Money. I walk to the mini fridge, grab a Choice Cherry Gold, take my phone and call the most important man that has ever been in my life next to my dad.

I hit *Send*, and before it even finishes one ring, I hear the tenderest, yet roughest voice I've ever known.

"Char-coal, are you okay?"

"No, Cash, I'm not, but I'll survive."

"Does that mean I need to get on the road?"

I pause for a moment, close my eyes, and begin to speak.

"No, Cash Money, as much as my heart is saying yes, I'm going to do this alone. I'll be home in a few days anyways."

"Aight, Char-coal, but if you change your mind, you better call me."

"I will. I want you to know that the Kluft girls are here for me. They didn't even go out tonight; instead, they helped me come out of the darkness. We're actually going to watch a movie in a little bit."

He starts to snicker. "Let me guess. *Sweet Home Alabama*, right?"

"You're a freakin' genius! You know that's my favorite! Gotta love when the good ol' country boy gets the girl instead of some Yankee." At that moment, I realize what I have just said, and it sounds like my damn life.

"Char-coal, I need you to do me a favor. I don't want you to be alone. I don't know what this shit is with Joe and Dylan, but I don't want a chance for Joe to try something else. Promise me if you leave your dorm, you won't be alone!"

"I don't think Georgia is going to let me out of her sight, but you have my word. I won't. Cash, I hope I can do this. I mean, this alone thing."

"Char, you are stronger than you give yourself credit for. Most people would have lost it by now."

I interrupt him, "No, Cash, you're wrong. I'm not strong. You are what keeps me together. I just put up a good front."

Cash and I finish our conversation, and I promise to call him if I change my mind. I know that I can't. I have to prove to myself that I do not need a guy, even if he is the one constant in my life. Through thick and thin, Cash Money is my rock, and I know more than anything that the love I have for him runs deeper than any river. I feel his love moving within my veins.

Chapter 2

After finishing *Sweet Home Alabama*, I decide it's time to hit the hay. I'm emotionally and physically worn out. I excuse myself from Tori's room and make my way down the hall. I go into my room, grab my toothbrush, and move toward the bathroom when I see Georgia.

"Hey, Char, you gonna be okay tonight, or do you want me to stay with ya?"

Her words bring forth a monsoon of emotion that I have tried to bury over the past hour, but I put up the wall in front of her as well.

"I'll be aight. If I need ya, you're just a few feet away."

She looks at me like I'm full of shit. "Okay, but I'm here if you change your mind."

At the same time, we turn on the water and brush our teeth in silence. When we finish, she gives me a hug and we go to our rooms.

I walk into my quiet room, pull back the covers, and turn on the TV. I flip through the channels and don't see much of anything. I decide on CMT and set my alarm for practice in the morning.

I toss and turn. I look at the clock. One o'clock… two o'clock… I finally drift off to sleep. Sleep that soon awakens me to reality with thoughts of Dylan, Joe, Cash, Piper, and everyone that I love.

My eyes snap open. I can hear my heart beating out of my chest, and I feel like I'm about to hyperventilate. Quickly, I sit up and tell myself that it's just a nightmare.

Dylan isn't here. Joe isn't going to bother me. Cash, Piper, and everyone else are fine.

The deceit and sadness I felt earlier is replaced with anger, and I want to walk my ass over to Irvin to give Joe a piece of my mind. *Don't Charley. That's a horrible idea, and Cash will kill you.* No matter how much I try to shake this feeling, I can't.

Before I realize what I am doing, my feet hit the floor, and I slide on my Ariats. I grab my keys and hustle down the stairs before someone notices me. I open the door, and the cool winter air hits my face and brings me back to reality. What the hell am I doing? As I walk around outside the dorm, I see someone approaching me. Tears start to fall as I realize who it is. Joe.

I turn as fast as I can, but I'm not quick enough. He catches my arm, and the smell of Jack Daniels is still on his breath. He doesn't seem to be drunk anymore. He must have drunk himself back to sobriety. I keep my head down, because I don't want to look into those make-you-wanna-melt eyes. If I do, I'm a goner.

"Squirrel, please listen to me. It's not what you think."

That one statement pulls me out of my thoughts, and I take a deep breath before letting harsh words escape my mouth.

"What I think? What the hell, Joe? I trusted you, and guess what? You are no better than Dylan! In fact, you're worse. You KNEW the entire time and didn't bother telling me. What kind of person are you? Oh, wait. I don't even think I can call you a human being because they have feelings, dammit!"

Joe keeps his grip on my arm as his eyes meet mine. He looks as if he is trying to find the right words to say, and that is all I need. I pull my arm from his and begin to walk back to Kluft, giving him one final statement to think about.

"When you grow a pair and decide to be the man that I thought you were, then we can talk. Until then, you can kiss my sweet Southern ass!" I grab the doorknob and stomp up the stairs. Lightening my feet just a tad so I do not wake everyone, I tiptoe down the hall and slide back into my bed.

As I pull the covers over my head, my phone begins to beep. I check to see who it might be at this time of night, and my stomach begins to do somersaults.

Dylan: Hope study day has been eventful. Just remember, I always have the upper hand.

My breath quickens, tears begin to silently fall down my cool cheeks, and my hands begin to quiver. What do I say? Do I not say anything? It looks like it's time to take my own advice and grow a pair.

Trying to steady my trembling fingers, I hit *Reply.*

Me: Eventful? Oh yeah, it's been eventful all right. I hope u sleep well at night motherfucker because 1 of these days ur gonna get what's coming to u!

Dylan: Such a potty mouth, what happened to sweet little Charley?

I can feel the heat begin to rise within my soul. I have got to end this madness somehow. I'm tired of being scared. Dylan is going down. You can count on that. I give him another quick reply because I don't want him to have the last word.

Me: U, asshole, that's what happened, but know this. U DON'T OWN ME! Now leave me alone. I have practice n a few hours.

I knew that last comment would leave him speechless. He thought he had taken away more than just my virginity. He tried to take away the one sport I love, but I have that back. Now it's time to create a plan...one that includes the Grassy Pond Aquatic Center (GPAC.)

There is no reply, just as I expected. I close my eyes, roll over, and smile. 1 point = Charley, 0 points = Dylan.

As I'm falling into a deep sleep, I hear the sound I hate the most. That damn alarm clock. Groggy, that is exactly what I am. I feel like I'm in a fog and can't see with my eyes or head. I know I have to roll out of these warm covers and face the reality of last night. What the hell was I thinking going outside? What if I see Joe today? What if Dylan texts again? I shake my head and throw back the covers, just as there is a knock at the door. Georgia. I grab my bag, and we make our way to the pool.

The pool. Water therapy is exactly what I need. I remove my Cash Money necklace and lock it inside my locker. I grab my cap and goggles and just about sprint to the pool. If I can't be at the club or in a tree, then this is the next best thing.

Coach's eyes meet mine, and she begins to say something, but blows the whistle for warm-ups to begin instead. We stretch and then begin the 500-meter choice. I scoop my cap into the water before placing it on my head and then position my goggles and dive into the cool, refreshing water.

As my body hits the water, it's as if my mind begins to turn, and I begin to relive every event from last night. Before I know what's going on, Coach is standing above my lane, splashing in the water and blowing her whistle.

"Charley, damn, honey, are you all right? I mean, I don't usually let words slip like that, but you've been on fire since you went into the water. I was afraid you were gonna have a heart attack out there."

As I get out of the pool to grab a drink of water, I reply, "I'll be aight, Coach. It was just a rough night, and not like you're thinkin' either. Study Day turned into a nightmare that I've been trying to escape for over a year. No matter what, it keeps rearing its ugly head right in my face."

"Well, obviously you didn't have a normal Study Day, or you would have puked by now. Seriously, if you need to talk, I'm here. I don't judge either," she responds as she wraps her arms around me.

"Thanks, Coach."

We pull apart, and she calls the next set. This set is a killer, but I'm ready. It's time to work out this rollercoaster of emotions in a place I know as home.

After practice, we all shower in the locker room and make our way to the café for breakfast before exams begin. Now that I'm out of the water, my nerves are starting to get the best of me. It must be written all over my face, because as we get ready to enter the café doors, Georgia looks at me and smiles. I nod, put on my big girl panties, and hold my head high.

We enter the café, and I scan the lacrosse table for Joe. I'm not sure how this will play out, especially after our late night meeting. I notice he's not there, and I shrug it off. I guess he's feeling the aftermath of all that Jack.

I grab my plate and make my way through the line. I feel the need for bacon, and I mean a lot of it. As I'm fixin' my plate, Tori pipes in.

"Damn, Charley, did they kill one hog just for you?"

"You know me. I lovvvvveee bacon. I swear I'd wear it as perfume if they had it!"

"That's gross! But then again, I bet it would call in the male species!" She laughs. "Speaking of which, look what the bacon dragged in."

Joe. That's what the bacon dragged in. His eyes meet mine, and I quickly turn away. I make my way over to our table and pull out my chair. Before I can sit, Joe is standing in front of me.

"We need to talk."

"No, we don't. Now move, asshole!"

Joe takes a step back as people begin to stare.

"We will talk, Squirrel." Tori begins to stand and has that 'open a can of whoop ass' look written all over her face. "You can slow your roll, Tori, because I'm not pushing her, but we will talk eventually."

He looks at me, turns, and walks away. As I watch him leave, I feel a piece of my heart break. Not because I'm in love with Jackalope Joe, but because I've lost a friend.

One that not only knows my darkest secrets, but Dylan's as well.

Chapter 3

After breakfast, I rush back to my room. It's time for a last minute cram session before biology. I send Cash a text to let him know I survived the night and will call him right after the exam.

Other than my blast with fresh air and Joe last night, I've not been alone. Needless to say, I have a gang of Kluft girls that go everywhere with me. If people didn't know better, they would probably think we are up to no good.

I enter the biology lecture hall with Dr. Deal right behind me. He takes the stack of exams and passes them out. I inhale a deep breath of fresh air, say a prayer, and let the knowledge I have flow from my fingertips. After finishing the exam, I take a brief moment to review my answers, because isn't that what all good students do? I quietly turn in my paper and march out of the room.

As I exit the building, I can't help but frown when I look at the spot where Joe would wait for me. Today he's not here, and if I had to do it all again, I don't know if I would change it.

As I walk back to my room alone, I call Cash.

"Hey, Char-coal, how are you this morning?"

"I'm hanging in there. I didn't sleep much last night, but I kicked ass at practice this morning."

"That's good and all, but what aren't you tellin' me? Remember, I can read your mind, or at least know when you aren't tellin' me everything. And, are you alone?"

"Yes, but I just finished my exam. That's why I called you on the way, so settle down. There's something I need to tell you, but first let me get to my room. Who knows who's listening around here?" I laugh, but it's cut short by Cash.

"What the hell, Char? This shit is serious! Do you know that I haven't slept at all? I've been worried sick. You want to do this alone, and I'm letting you. It might kill me in the process, so don't joke, okay? I love you too much to let something happen to you, and right now I'm worried to death."

"I'm sorry. I just have to laugh, because if I don't, I'll cry. I didn't sleep much either. Hold on a sec. I'm almost to my room."

I rummage for my key out of my backpack and open the door. I throw my bag onto the bed and sit down.

"Okay, so here's what you need to know. I had a nightmare last night. I woke up upset, but then I was more pissed than scared. Before I knew what I was doing, I was outside alone. I kinda realized it was a bad idea when the cold air woke me up, but by then it was too late, because Joe was out there. He wanted to talk, but I pretty much told him to grow a pair first and then we'd talk. Later, as I was almost asleep, I got a text from Dylan."

"Char, I think I need to come down there. If anyone's going to jail, it's going to be me and not you."

"No, you're not. See, I wanted to march my ass over to Irvin and punch the shit out of Joe, but then I realized what good would that do? He's hiding something. As much as I don't like it, I think Dylan is holding something against him, and I'm going to figure it out. And... I'm gonna put a stop to Dylan, but we're gonna have to have a bullet-proof plan."

I take a breath, and Cash takes a minute to respond.

"Char-coal, are you sure you want to go up against the devil?"

"You bet your fine ass I do! I pulled a card on him last night in those texts. I told him I had practice this morning. He didn't text anything back after that. He knows that I'm stronger than he gives me credit. I wanna take him down, Cash Money, but I need your help. Are you with me?"

"If this is what you want, then damn right I'm with ya. Haven't I always been?"

"Thanks, Cash Money." It's moments like these that I wish I were safe in the arms of Cash Money in the club in Grassy Pond.

"Char, have you talked to Piper? 'Cause I think we might have a problem."

As soon as he says those words, I don't need an explanation. Joe. That's the problem. Piper is head over heels for Jackalope Joe, and how in the hell am I gonna tell her that he's full of shit?

"I'll worry about that when I get home. I finish my exams tomorrow, but they are having a Christmas Party on our hall Friday night. I'm going to stay and try to have a good time. Then, I'll be home Saturday morning."

"You want me to come and be your date?"

I squish my lips together and move them from side to side as I contemplate my answer.

"As much as I want to say yes, I'm gonna say no. Let me try this independent thing a little while longer."

"Aight, well, let me know if you change your mind."

"I will. I better get ready for my next exam. Love you, Cash Money."

"Love you, Char-coal."

I press *End* and sit on the edge of the bed. My next exam… freshman seminar. I drop my face into my hands as I rest my elbows on my knees. Oh shit. I totally forgot about the collaboration session for our exam. Fifteen minutes until I have to face Jackalope Joe and have an actual conversation in front of Dr. Cope. I. Sit. And. Pray.

Chapter 4

I wait until the last minute to walk across campus…
alone. Stupid, yes, I know. Everything seems to stand still
as I tread across the train tracks and glance at the front lawn
where this nightmare all began. When I look at the front
lawn, I can't help but relive the first day on campus.
Memories from the moment I saw those make-you-wanna-
melt eyes to how I couldn't wait to press my sweet lips to
his come to mind. Little did I know those lips would be
full of deceit and cause so much pain.

I pull myself from my thoughts and make my way into
Dr. Cope's classroom, instantly locking eyes with
Jackalope Joe. I quickly look the opposite way to find a
seat, but the only available one is my usual chair right
beside a guy I love to hate. Although for some reason, I
want to have faith in him.

Dr. Cope begins class, and several students finish their
projects. It's doomsday when she drags me from the
thoughts running within my head as I hear her call our
names. WTH?!

"Joe and Charley, you seemed to have created a strong
bond and learned a lot about each other this semester.
Honestly, I haven't seen a pair with your type of
connection, ever. Can you tell the class what caused it?"

Joe and I sit in our seats, unsure of who needs to speak
first. I decide I'll be the one to grow a pair, as usual.

I stand and walk to the front of the room. Looking
directly into the eyes of someone I thought I could trust, I
speak the truth.

"Dr. Cope, Joe and I had a connection long before we met at Southern. Little did I know that was the cause until recently. Joe and I worked well because we had trust. It's almost as if we had been long-lost friends. My advice is to make sure you truly know the people who claim to support you, because in the end, all you have are true friends."

I don't break eye contact with Jackalope Joe as I make my way back to my seat. I wait for him to make a comment, but he doesn't. Just like I thought, he's not a true friend; he's a complete lie.

Dr. Cope concludes class and gives each of us a hug on the way out the door. I try to make a beeline across campus, but it's no use. Joe catches me.

"Look, Squirrel. I'm sorry. I really am." He continues to talk as I increase my speed while I walk back to Kluft. "Stop and listen for just a minute, please!"

I stop abruptly and face him. "What?!"

"I need you to hear me out. It's not like you think. Well, it is, but it isn't." I look at him puzzled. "Yes, originally, it was just a big payoff from Dylan, but then I met you. I knew the moment you opened your mouth with the Cougar Charley comment that it was going to be different."

"Whatever, Joe." He grabs my arm as I turn to walk away. "Let go of me!" I grit through my teeth.

"No, Squirrel, please listen."

I stop. "I'm listening." I pull my arm from his grip, cross my arms, and wait.

"This might take a while. Can we go somewhere?"

"Sure, but I will not be alone with you. Let me text Georgia."

Me: Joe wants to talk. Can you come outside?

GA: U got it!

Joe and I stand in silence as we wait for Georgia. I see her short self coming out the door and toward us. She might be short, but she looks like she's six feet tall and ready to beat some ass. She's on a mission, that's for sure. Gah, I love her!

Georgia quickly approaches us. "Joe, what do you have to say?"

As we make our way to the picnic table that has so many memories of Joe and me, Georgia laughs as if she can't believe it.

"Don't you think for one minute that going to sit at a ratty, old picnic table is gonna fix this! I don't care if this *is* where it all started!" she says as if she were spitting fire.

"Georgia, I just need to talk, that's all. Yeah, Squirrel and I had a lot of great moments here, but at least it's quiet. Hopefully, everyone won't be in our business," Joe replies, staring at Georgia.

She takes a step toward him, crosses her arms, and dares him to test her.

Joe takes a step back and retreats from Georgia. He sits at the table and motions for us to as well.

"I think we'll stand!" Georgia states and I nod in agreement.

Joe looks completely out of his element, but begins explaining himself. This should be interesting.

"Okay, here it is, but let me start by saying that I was a different person when I made this deal."

Georgia and I look at each other and roll our eyes.

Joe fidgets as he searches for words. "I met Dylan during Senior Week at Myrtle Beach. He seemed like a good guy and was the life of the party. I got pretty wasted one night and told him my darkest secrets. Then, we realized we had a few things in common and became friends on Facebook. I didn't think much about it because I was having a really hard time with Lucy. My parents pretty much kicked me to the curb after I got in trouble at school. I couldn't do anything right. If Gran hadn't taken me in, who knows where I would be by now. I'd probably be in jail. I made some really bad choices. Gran kept her faith in me and helped me find Southern. They took a gamble on me because of my record."

As he takes a breath, I put in my two cents.

"So, what does that have to do with me?" I can't help but wonder what deep secret they share.

"Okay, I hadn't heard much from Dylan all summer. Right before school started, he asked me if I was in need of some extra cash. He knew how hard it was on Gran and me financially. I listened to him. He pretty much told me that his ex was coming to Southern, and he wanted to make sure that she had a friend. He wanted to know the details of her college career and didn't want another guy getting his girl.

I didn't think much about it, and then he offered to pay me a good bit of change. I was desperate. Without my parents, college was tough on Gran. I didn't think I had a choice."

"Yes, you did, Joe! No matter how much money he offered, spying into someone's privacy isn't right!"

"Charley, he made it look like he was just keeping tabs. Like you two were taking a break."

"Let me ask you something." He nods. "You were talking to him the day I scared you in this very spot. Weren't you?" He nods again. "You're an ass, you know that! I trusted you! But, the sad part is you already knew!"

"I'm sorry, Squirrel. I realized he wasn't who he said he was until too late. By that point, I was too far in it, and I didn't know how to correct this mistake with Dylan or you. When you told me everything in the Jeep, I honestly didn't know any of that. I could have killed him for using me."

"As much as I'd love to just forgive you, I can't right now. I need time, but let me tell you something. You could have told me. You saw how he bullied my friends, you, and me, and you still didn't talk. I just can't understand it. Georgia, I'm done here. Let's go."

We turn around and I do not look over my shoulder. As soon as we hit second floor Kluft, the waterworks begin, because no matter how mad I want to be at Joe, my heart needs to believe him. The question is, do I follow my head or my heart?

Georgia stops me and pulls me in for a tight hug. I try to hold in the emotions, but it's no use. A loud sob erupts from my lungs, and I fall apart in her arms. Before I realize what is going on, every girl on my floor is huddled around me and not letting go.

After what feels like an eternity, I pull myself together. Using my sleeve, I wipe away the salty tears.

"I'm so sorry, y'all. You shouldn't have to deal with this mess."

"Charley, you're one of us, and we will not let you sink. We are a family here, and we will keep you afloat until you can sail on your own," Caroline says, as she puts her arm around my shoulder.

"Thanks, I think I'm going to take a nap. Maybe it will help me get over this shit."

"I think some retail therapy is just what the doctor ordered!" Anna says with a smirk.

I know exactly what they are thinking. We need new attire for the Kluft Christmas Party. Guess it's a trip to The Mills whether I want to or not. I do remember something about an ugly sweater.

Chapter 5

After trying to rest for a few hours, we pile into the Love Machine and head to The Mills. Before we get there, we make a detour at the Goodwill to find a tacky Christmas sweater. You know the ones that elementary school teachers or your grandma wears.

As we all pile into the van, it's kinda an uncomfortable silence. I don't know if it's just me, or if they are terrified to say anything. Anna begins to sing to "Royals" on the radio, and I fall in sync with her. She looks my direction and smiles. This must be what they are waiting on, because within seconds, we are all singing at the top of our lungs.

Each song bleeds into the next until the commercial break. We laugh at Hayden's rendition of "Roar" by Katy Perry. Then, she begins to actually roar like a lion. You just never know what that girl is going to do!

We roll into the Goodwill and peruse the aisles with one mission in mind. Tacky. Horrific. Grandma-inspired Christmas sweaters. The funnier the better.

Within minutes, we find one that fits each of our personalities, and of course, mine has Rudolph on it! We spend two dollars apiece, and then move on to a little finer shopping, The Mills.

We roll in on two wheels and pile out. We decide to take the tacky sweaters and make a sexy outfit, which I'm wondering if it is even possible, considering my blue sweater is equipped with huge snowballs for buttons and the entire sleigh crew embroidered on the front. We know our best bets are Wet Seal, Charlotte Russe, and Forever 21. Which do we hit up first?

We walk into Charlotte Russe. Nothing is really standing out, so we make our way to Wet Seal. I see exactly what I'm looking for when I walk inside, a white tulle lace mini skirt! It will take me from frumpy granny to hot in two seconds! Now, only if I had a new pair of boots!

We spend the next two hours trying to find everyone the perfect accessories to complement the tackiness they bought at the Goodwill.

I continue to look for a new pair of boots and realize that it's a lost cause. I need to go to Lebo's like yesterday!

"Y'all, I need a new pair of boots. Wanna know where I do my shoppin'?" I say as I look through a rack of shirts.

"Hell yeah, Charley! I'd love to see a few cowboys while we're at it," Hayden states as she attempts her best Southern drawl, which isn't successful.

After Tori and Anna complete their outfits, it's on to Lebo's. As we walk into the store, the smell of leather tickles my nose. I. Love. It. I can feel the excitement of looking through my favorite store for a new pair of boots.

Glancing at my friends, I can tell they are a little overwhelmed.

"Y'all, welcome to my world! Don't y'all just love it? Gah, I could stay in here all day!"

"Char, this is crazy! I didn't know there was this much country shit, but I do have to say…that tall, dark and 100% country boy near the jeans is H-O-T!" Anna states with her Yankee attitude.

"Shhh, Anna, he's gonna hear you!" I reply as I cut my eyes to her.

After I take a moment, I glance over to see the eye candy, and damn, he's fine! Oh, and that ass is perfect! I can't help but laugh at the fact I've just given the Kluft girls a new experience. I pull myself from the hot country boy and make my way to the boots on the wall. It takes me all of two seconds to know which pair I want. They are absolutely perfect except for the price. But, good boots are expensive.

I pick up the display of a tan with blue design Rouge Ariats. They are gorgeous, and then I look at the price tag. Two hundred and nine dollars. *Crap!* I take a moment to rationalize the situation. I haven't bought a new pair of shoes in over a year, and I'm going home tomorrow. Yeah, I think it's time to splurge. Nothing like a new pair of boots to brighten your spirit!

The sales associate walks over and asks if she can help. I don't need any help. I just need a size eight.

"Yes, ma'am, I need these in a size eight, please."

"Sure." She turns and goes to the storeroom and reappears with a box that holds my new love.

She opens the box, and it's as if I've never seen anything so beautiful. She hands me one, and I slide off my boot and try it on. *Perfect. Absolutely Perfect.* I tell her that I want them and then take a moment to look around the store. I notice a pair of Tuff Jeans on the sales rack for less than forty bucks. Those have my name on them, and then I check the tops. I find the perfect pearl snap. It's brown plaid with just enough blue and white. It's embellished on the back with wings and a heart.

Something about the heart and wings draws me in like it's talking to me. I have to have it. I grab it and pay before any more damage is done.

As I make my way to the register, the hot country boy that Anna was drooling over gives me a nod and smile. I return the smile. I do not want to hear this total.

"That will be two hundred eighty-seven dollars and thirty-five cents." I break out the plastic and swipe. *I hope my mama doesn't kill me.*

Everyone is still looking around, but it's more like they are looking at all the fine country boys that walk into the store. I gotta get them outta here before they get the courage to say what they are thinking.

"Y'all ready?" I ask.

"Damn, Charley, why have you been holding out on us?" Tori responds.

I just shrug my shoulders, smile, and let out a giggle. "What am I gonna do with y'all?"

We make our way back to Southern and get ready for the party. We have a lot to do and not a lot of time. Luckily, the girls did a little prep work while I tried to clear my head.

Georgia and I finish decorating the entrance, while Caroline checks on her famous PJ, and Anna and Tori play DJ. Within thirty minutes, we have our hallway looking like Santa and his elves came to visit.

Hayden and Sarah arrive because they are honorary Kluft girls, and of course, they aren't empty-handed. They have pizza and a case of Bud Light.

"Please tell me you picked up the pizza in that get-up?" I ask as I add one last piece of tape to a streamer.

"You know it! Who wouldn't want me all wrapped up as a present?" Hayden says assuredly.

"You ain't right, but I'm about to starve!"

We all pile onto the middle of the floor, eating straight from the box and each popping a top on a Bud Light. Nothing like pizza and beer.

One by one we excuse ourselves to put our hot twist on our tacky Christmas sweater.

I enter my room and turn on Pandora to Today's Country. I sing to myself as I get ready. I put on my sweater, skirt, and take my time doing my makeup and adding accessories. Then, I slide on my new boots. I look into the mirror, and for the first time, I see a girl with strength and courage in her eyes. I can do this.

I text Cash a quick pic and wait for a reply, because there is always a reply. Instead, I hear "Crash my Party" blaring through my phone.

"Hey, Cash Money."

"You know Santa's leaving you coal, don't ya?"

"What do you mean? I'm on his good list this year."

"Well, if you can take something that hideous and make it look that hot, there's no way you're still on his good list!"

"You ain't right! I've done nothin' wrong," I say in my sweetest Southern drawl.

"I know you haven't, but you sure are KILLING me! I just keep telling myself twenty-four more hours! Then, it's you and me."

"I know, but I really think this has been good for me. It's like a brand new me."

"Charley, just make sure that new you includes me."

"Cash Money, there's nothing that can keep me away from you."

"I'll let you get to the party. I can't wait to see you tomorrow. I love you, Char-coal."

"I love you too, Cash Money."

After placing my phone onto the dresser, I take another look into the mirror. It's time for one night where I don't worry about Dylan or Joe. It's time to have a little fun with the girls.

Tori and Anna put on a little R&B Christmas music to get the night going. We all drink Caroline's PJ from Christmas Solo cups. Before long, this Christmas party turns into just a typical Southern Friday night.

After the third cup of PJ, I realize that I should have stopped about two cups ago. I look at Georgia, and she has the same look on her face. What do we do? We refill our cups for one more, then another, and then another.

Before I know it, I'm drunk as a skunk. I try to sit down but that makes it worse. Everything is spinning. I do not like this feeling.

"Get your butts up, girls! Only way to sober up is to eat some bread and dance your ass off!" Tori yells.

"Yes, ma'am!" I slur as Georgia and I use each other to stand up. We grab what pizza is left and inhale it and then drink a bottle of water.

Tori has now turned the Christmas music to Hank's style music. It's almost as if everyone knows where the party is because every athlete on campus is on Kluft second floor except... Joe. *I wonder where he is?*

As soon as the thought enters, I see those piercing blue eyes walking down the hallway. I begin to shake my head no, but he completely ignores me. He heads straight for me and begins to grab my hand when Georgia puts in her two cents.

"Uh, no, you don't! She's done with you." She takes her time so the words aren't slurred.

"No. She's. Not. I need to make this right before tomorrow morning. Now, if you'll excuse us."

I can feel my heart rate increase, and the pool of tears build. This was supposed to be a night without this mess, and yet again, Dylan seems to be in control.

Joe looks at me with pleading eyes, and I nod yes. I glance back over my shoulder at Georgia. We have a secret code. Come and get me in five.

I walk with him into my room and close the door.

"Please don't cry, Squirrel." He tries to brush away the tears, but I push away his hand instead.

"Keep your hands off me. Got it?"

"Yeah, please tell me you thought about what I told you? Tell me you forgive me. I can't leave for a month knowing that I ruined the best relationship I've ever had other than with Gran. I can't lose you. I'll take whatever you can give."

"Joe, right now I really want to forgive you, but I would rather be angry. What you did is unforgiveable. You're no better than Dylan! I just can't right now."

His eyes begin to glisten, and I know I've hurt him. That's what I want. I want to hurt him as much as he has hurt me.

"Squirrel, even though you didn't give me the answer I wanted, I believe there is hope in your words. I hope you have a great break, and when you decide I'm worthy of being forgiven, call me no matter what time."

He takes a step away from me and walks out the door. As it closes, tears stream down my face, and I'm completely sober now.

Within seconds, Georgia is in my room. She has two glasses in her hands. We sit in the floor and get sloppy drunk, while I relive every moment of my past: the good, the bad, and the totally fucked up.

At some point, the music dies down and people retire to their rooms. I stumble into my bed with my ugly sweater acting as pajamas and go to sleep because I have no fight in me at this point. Tomorrow is another day.

Chapter 6

Holy shit! My head feels like it's throbbing, and my ringing phone sounds like needles penetrating my skull. Hungover. That is what it is and why I'm not a fan. I do believe this is the only time in my life that I haven't wanted Luke Bryan to crash my party because undoubtedly I partied too much last night. As I reach for my phone, I feel like my arm weighs two tons and I'm totally off balance. I know that ringtone and who's on the other side. It makes me smile, which takes all efforts at this point in the day.

"Hey, Cash Money," I say groggily.

"Char-coal, are you hungover?" he questions.

"Uh huh, I feel like shit on the bottom of a horse's hoof."

He begins to laugh. "Well, that's one way to put it. You gonna be able to drive home today?"

"I sure hope so. We've got a lot to talk about, and, oh gosh, hold on." I throw my phone onto the bed and make a mad dash to the bathroom. I barely make it to the porcelain throne before spilling all the contents from my stomach. *Better. Much better.* I wash my hands and take a few deep breaths before returning to my room to finish my conversation. "Sorry."

"You feel better?"

"Yup, still got a headache that won't quit, but what I wouldn't kill for a Cajun filet biscuit about now."

"And Bo Rounds? Sweet tea? Bo Berry Biscuits? Do you want me to keep goin'?" Cash snickers.

"My mouth is watering thanks to you! If I ever decide to do this again, remind me not to! I don't know why people think this is fun. But, hell, mine was just 'cause Joe showed up again."

"Whoa! What did you say? Hold on and let me get this straight. Joe showed up, and you got drunk? What the hell, Char? I'm not there!"

"Don't get your panties in a tangle just yet! I got piss-ass drunk with Georgia right by my side after he left. I'm good. Now, I'm gonna get off here and try to act like I'm not hungover. I'll text you before I leave, but just so you know, the Kluft girls are going to Hank's tonight and I know them well enough to know that I'm gonna have to have a damn good excuse not to go."

"Char, do what you want to, but be careful. Call and let me know what you decide. 'Cause I wanna go hunting this afternoon if you're not coming home."

"Don't let that stop ya. You know it wouldn't me." I smirk because he knows that is one hundred percent the truth.

"Call me, Char. Love you."

"Love you."

I hang up the phone and fall back onto the bed. A shower can wait until this morning nap is complete, and I pray I wake up minus a headache.

My nap is interrupted by a light knocking on my door. I roll out of bed and realize that my body isn't having an out-of-body experience anymore, and the headache is now a dull constant as opposed to a constant throb. I twist the knob and find Georgia standing there with her hair looking a hot mess. If I didn't know better, I'd say she'd been rolling around in the sheets with someone, but that is not Georgia's style. She has high standards, and one-night stands are not included.

We don't speak. She just enters and makes herself comfortable on my bed after grabbing a Choice Cherry Gold and a box of Cheez-Its.

"So, Char, do you remember last night? I mean, I hope you remember what happened before we got piss-ass drunk. I'm sorry for that, but you needed it."

"Yeah, I remember Joe, if that's what you mean. I've got a question, though. Why did you let him take me in here alone? I just didn't think you would do that."

"I wanted to stop him, but the look on his face and those eyes told me more than I ever wanted to know. Plus, I figured that if he was on our territory he wouldn't do anything. I was giving him five minutes, and then I was gonna beat down the door if he didn't let me in. Instead, he excused himself like a gentleman."

Gentleman. That word struck a nerve. It wasn't long ago that I used the same term to describe Joe. A gentleman... my ass.

"Char, I know you have been through a lot, but I want to know what you have planned over break. If you aren't doing much, maybe we can meet up or something?"

"Girl, 'Bama is a haul from here, but let's see what we can figure out. Oh, and I think I'm going to try to head out before long. What about you?"

"I think I'm going to Hank's tonight and then on the road first thing in the morning." Georgia puts back the Cheez-Its onto the shelf before making her way to get ready.

I stand and gaze at myself in the mirror. I look like death warmed over. Maybe a hot shower will do the trick.

Once I take care of the three *S's* and put myself together, I begin to take on the task of packing. The question is, if I'm going home for a month, what do I need? What's at home? I'm not packing up this room to bring it back in four weeks. I decide to take the necessities and worry about the rest when I get home. Worst case scenario involves Piper and me shopping at Northlake.

As I'm packing, I come across the squirrel charm that Joe gave me at homecoming. I hold it tight within my grip and pray that he is good and this is just a test for all of us.

I place it inside the zipper compartment of my cosmetic bag and toss the bag over my shoulder. I walk into the hallway and begin to make my way to the car when Caroline walks out of her room.

"Where do you think you're goin'?" she asks with her hands on her hips.

"To put my bag in the car. I'm not leaving just yet."

"Well, you know tonight's Hank's, and I can't believe you'd leave without going. It's going to be epic. Last night at Hank's before break. Please tell me you aren't gonna miss it?"

"Well, I had planned on missing it. I..." Caroline quickly interrupts me.

"Listen, Char. I know life's been kinda shitty lately, but it's our last night before we all leave. Let's go let our hair down. Y'all don't have practice or class. It'll just be fun with the girls. Who knows, you might meet some hot baseball guy?" she says as she nudges me.

"Whatever. I'll think about it, but I'm just getting ready to go home."

"Okay, but it will be fun. I promise."

I look at Caroline like she's an idiot. "Caroline, hun, Hank's is always fun. I just want to get home and release all this stress with my Marlin 30/30. There's a doe, buck, or even a tin can calling my name!"

I walk past her, down the stairs to my car, and pop the trunk. Using a few extra minutes, I think about what I want to do. I want to go home, but a night out would be great. When I think about that, I think about last night. That was not fabulous like I had planned. Maybe I should stay around. Heck, who wants to have their last night of the semester end in tears, heartache, and the worst hangover of their life? I think a night at Hank's is just the cure.

Taking my bag, I unzip it and remove my cosmetic bag and walk back upstairs. I'm going to have a good time with the girls tonight, and no guys are going to ruin it.

Chapter 7

Tucking my bag underneath my arm, I make my way back up the stoop and onto Kluft second floor. The girls are chillin' in the hallway, and Caroline is grinning from ear to ear.

"Not a word, Caroline. Not a word."

"I didn't say a thing," she says in her sweet Southern drawl.

"Yeah, whatever. You are dying to say I told ya so!"

"What can I say? I love when redneck meets ghetto fabulous."

Tori chimes in, "Ya know, Char, if you can come up with shit like that, they're going to hire you for one of those damn Budweiser commercials. Then, we'll say we knew you when." I just shake my head.

I take a moment to send Cash, Piper, and Tessa a quick text telling them that I will be home tomorrow. The Kluft girls spend the remainder of the day watching chick flicks, eating leftover pizza, and preparing for an epic night at Hank's. I'm hoping to make this a night I don't forget, so no alcohol for me.

I glance in my closet. *What to wear? What to wear?* Heck, it's Hank's. It's not like it really matters, and I have no one to impress. I pull a pair of Miss Me jeans, a solid purple tank, and my Ariats. I brush through my hair and apply a little mascara, blush, and lip gloss, and I'm ready to leave.

"Dang, Char, you're gonna kill them tonight," Anna says as I walk out of my room.

I stop and look her way. She can't be serious. "Um, what are you talking about? I'm just dressed like I always do at home."

Hayden begins to laugh, and it can't be good. "Well, no wonder Cash doesn't want anyone to get near you, 'cause if I looked that good in a pair of jeans and a plain tank, I'd shake my money maker for all it's worth!" She winks.

"Seriously, Hayden? I just grabbed something from the closet. I'm not trying to impress anyone tonight."

"That's where you're wrong. Those baseball guys are gonna be all over you tonight. Just watch."

We turn up the music, and everyone partakes in a few more beverages before we pile into the Love Machine and make our way toward Hank's.

As usual, we roll in on two wheels, and nothing about this place has changed since our last visit. It's amazing how a run-down place that smells like skunked beer and cigarettes could be our second home. It's our escape from reality, like our sanctuary away from class, parents, drama, and the world outside these four walls.

I take a minute and check the rearview mirror. Smile. There's nothing in the pearly whites, and then I slide out of the driver's seat onto the gravel. I pat my pocket, making sure I have my ID.

Georgia makes it about halfway across the road before the pavement grows a foot and she's face-first on the ground. She starts to laugh hysterically, and I pull her up by her arms. Good thing this isn't a high-traffic road. She better slow her roll, or she's gonna be passed out before long.

We push through the glass door and past the bouncer who eyes me from head to toe as we make our way into Hank's. Of course, we form our usual beeline to the bathroom and the stall with no door.

"All right, ladies, what's the plan tonight? Who's getting a piece before they go home for a month?" Hayden questions. She scans all of us, and most have their hands raised, but Georgia and me. "Char, I hate to break it to you, but if you don't get a piece, it's your own damn fault. Georgia, we know you well enough to know that you're gonna have those hips rockin' the dance floor with one guy all night long."

I just shake my head. Sometimes being sober isn't fun. Hell, it never is, but tonight's about cutting lose and staying in control.

We make our way to the bar and order Bud Lights all around plus my water. Then, it's to the dance floor. The sound of Flo Rida's "Wild Ones" echoes through the speakers, and we know exactly what to do. We hit the dance floor and go hard. It's about us girls having a good time tonight. Here we don't have to worry about some ass trying to interrupt or put moves on us that we don't want. Hayden starts acting a fool by doing that damn sprinkler dance move, and I totally lose it. We all take turns goofing off and breaking out old school moves.

When Drake's "Started from the Bottom" comes across the speakers, we quit goofing off and start dancing our asses off. Before we know what's going on, the entire baseball team is surrounding us and enjoying the view. Songs bleed from one to the next. Once sweat begins to drip down my back, I pull my hair up into a messy bun and continue to enjoy the night.

By song number four, a smokin' hot baseball player has his strong hands wrapped around my waist. I swear I've just met Chipper Jones fifteen years ago! I continue to dance and take in the aroma of sweat and Dolce and Gabbana. Holy crap. I never thought those two things would go together. The songs change pace and begin to slow. I know I need to separate myself from him, because at this point, I'm not looking for someone new. As I start to pull away, he grabs my hand and tugs me close.

"Hey, Char, I'm Tucker, or can I call you Squirrel?" I must have looked like a damn deer in headlights because I completely froze right after he said it. No one calls me that but Joe. WTF? My breath begins to heighten, and I can feel sweat building under my arms. Tucker must have noticed as well. "Um, did I say something wrong? I thought that was your nickname?"

I swallow hard. "Well, that's what Joe calls me."

"So, is it okay if I call you that?" His eyes look as sincere as they can despite the amount of alcohol he has flowing in his veins. I shake my head no.

"I'd rather you didn't."

"All right, but just so you know, he's a complete idiot for letting you go that easy." Here we go. Another night with my drama. What do I do? I have to get him to shut up about Joe before I freakin' lose it. I take my hands and run them up his washboard stomach. I can feel every chiseled ab and indention. I look up at him, and he gets the point.

Not one more word about Joe. As the song comes to an end, he pulls me in close and lifts my chin. "Like I said, he's a fuckin' idiot," he says as his lips brush mine.

My mind takes a moment to focus on what is going on. Warm, soft, hungry lips are covering mine. Tucker pulls away from me and kisses my forehead as the next song, "Roar" by Katy Perry, begins to play. I start to laugh inside, thinking about Hayden. I glance at the Kluft girls who are obviously thinking the same thing. I smile at Tucker and make my way to them about the time the chorus begins, and we all sing at the top of our lungs.

I know it's near closing time, which means the one song that always ends a night at Hank's is about to be played. I push that thought to the back of my brain and just let loose for the next twenty minutes. When the first chord of "Let's Get It On" begins, I back away from the dance floor.

As I turn to walk away, intense blue eyes stare back at me. Joe. *Joe's here?* My heart begins to hurt. I want to forgive him, but I just can't. Not yet.

Joe gives me no option. He takes my hand and guides me back to the dance floor. Georgia looks like she is shooting darts straight at him. He ignores her and wraps his arms around me. I drop my head to his chest, and tears begin to fall. *Why can't my nightmare end? Why?*

We attempt to dance, but our worlds have stopped. He stands with his arms around my trembling body, and I look up to him as the song ends. Barely audible words escape his lips. "Squirrel, I'm here when you're ready."

I wipe the tears from my face as I pull myself from his embrace. I turn and leave him standing alone on the dance floor. The Kluft girls are waiting for me once I reach the door, and Georgia pulls me in for a hug. We exit Hank's and pile into the Love Machine, and I don't look back. As I take a deep breath, crank the van, and begin to pull out, I see Joe walking out of Hank's. Our eyes meet, and I turn my head as quickly as possible. I do not want to feel any connection to Joe, but my heart tells me otherwise.

We make it back to campus with the typical roadblock, walk up the stoop, and into bed in record time.

After crawling into bed, I send Cash a quick text. I roll over, close my eyes, and succumb to the exhaustion. Tomorrow is a new day.

Chapter 8

The morning light peers through my window and wakes me an hour before I'd like. I pull my sheets over my head and doze back off for another forty-five minutes.

I wake up to "Hell on Heels," Piper's ringtone.

"Hello," I croak.

"Hey, Char, you ain't on the road yet? We got shit to do, girl! I mean, I haven't seen you in what feels like forever! How's Joe?"

Damn, I'm not even awake now. How did I not tell Piper yet? "Um, good I guess."

"What do you mean? *Good?* What's wrong, Char?"

"Let's just say Joe's not on our team. Look. I don't want to get into it right now. I should be home by one. I'll see you then."

"Okay, you're kinda scaring me, but I'll meet you at the farm around two. That is unless you and Cash Money have other plans."

"I'm sure he's gonna be waiting, but you might as well come on over 'cause we all need to talk."

"Char, I'm no idiot. I know this has to do with the asshole of the century. He better not show his face while we're home. Be careful. I'll have Fun Dip and a Choice Cherry Gold waitin'."

"Sounds good. Bye, Piper."

We hang up, and I throw off the covers and sit for a minute. To take a shower or not? That is the question. Then, the aroma of Hank's hits my nostrils, and there is no doubt. Shower.

I decide not to waste much time on my wardrobe. I grab my new jeans, a long-sleeved white tee, boots, and veto drying my hair by putting on my favorite camo ball cap. Once I'm ready, the girls and I grab a bite to eat and all go our separate ways. I crank up the radio and the heat in the Honda. It feels like minutes instead of an hour when I realize that I've been lost in thought the majority of the way. Can we say dangerous? Note to self: focus while driving.

I pop in our drunk mix CD that Caroline always plays in her room while we drink PJ. It's a lot more comical to listen to while sober. Seriously, the country version of "Gin and Juice" and "The Monster" by Eminem? I can't help but laugh. It doesn't get any better when "Genie in a Bottle" by Christina Aguilera begins playing. What was she thinking? Oh, wait. She wasn't thinking because she was drunk.

I approach Grassy Pond, and nothing has changed since Thanksgiving. It's still stoplight after stoplight. I can't wait to hit that gravel road. I see the farm approaching and feel the butterflies within my stomach. For once, I'm excited and relieved to be home.

Turning off the ignition, I see Blue running toward me. As soon as I'm out of the car, he attacks me. "Yeah, boy, I've missed you, too." I rub behind his ears and then make my way to the house.

There's no need to hurry, because as I glance up, Tessa and Mama are in full out sprints. I giggle inside. Tessa wraps me in a tight embrace.

"Miss me much?" I smirk.

"Char, I swear. Mama and Dad have been workin' me to death on this farm. If you didn't get home soon, I might actually have had to take care of those stupid goats, not to mention sloppin' the hogs. Yuck!"

I should have known Tessa was more excited because that meant less work for her, but that's my sis, always missin' when a little hard work needs to be done.

"Hey, sweet girl, I'm glad you're home. Your dad's gone into town to get a few posts for the fence. I don't know what has gotten into that bull out there. It's like he just doesn't know which side he belongs," Mama says.

I open the trunk and grab my bags. Mama grabs my laundry basket, and we make our way into the house.

As I walk through the screen door, the sound of an F250 that I'd know anywhere rings in my ears. I smile and throw my bag at the bottom of the stairs. I do a one-eighty, press the screen door open, jump off the stairs, and run as fast as my legs will go to that perfect sound. Cash opens the door and steps out in one swift motion. He has on a pair of jeans, a white plaid pearl snap, camo hat, and boots. *Damn.* I jump straight into his arms and hold him as close as possible.

"Miss me much?" He winks.

I begin to laugh uncontrollably. "You know, I just used that line on Tessa." I pull him closer. He looks into my eyes, smiles with that damn dimple, and I feel complete. Cash Money makes me whole.

He finally puts me down when he hears the screen door open behind me. I turn around to see Tessa standing there with her hands on her hips. "Um, did y'all plan that?"

"Plan what, Tess?" I question as I straighten my long-sleeved white shirt. Then, it dawns on me. Jeans, white shirt, camo hat, and boots. Cash and I look like we planned our freakin' wardrobe.

"What can I say? Great minds think alike," Cash says as he slaps my ass while we walk toward the house. We go inside where Mama has lunch waiting.

As we are fixin' our plates, I hear the door open. I assume it's Dad, but soon realize that's a negative.

"Please tell me that you saved me some, Mama Number Two?!" Piper yells as she walks down the hallway.

I jump from my chair with a mouth half full of my mama's famous spaghetti and meet Piper as she turns the corner for the kitchen. I hurry up and swallow as we start talking like we haven't seen each other in years. Tessa, Cash and Mama completely ignore us. They've learned over the years that we have our own language, finish each other sentences, and take all of five minutes to fill in each other on the past few months of our lives.

"Well, I guess my Choice Cherry Gold and Fun Dip are no match for Mama Number Two's spaghetti." Piper places them onto the counter and grabs a plate. Then, she finds a seat next to Tessa.

"So, what's the dill, pickle?" Piper asks between bites.

"There's a party at the McCracken's farm tonight, and I thought maybe tomorrow we could all hang out at the club. Tessa, you can come, too," Cash says.

"Cash, I appreciate the offer, but I don't feel like little ol' Tess needs an invite. Dustin and I are planning on going mudding tomorrow."

"Muddin? Tess, you're going muddin' and didn't even think about inviting us? Have I been gone that long? I mean, we're a country boy and girls on the farm. HELLLOOOO!" I say.

"Um, I don't know about y'all, but mud and I don't mix! I'm good as long as I'm inside the truck, but I don't look this good to go and get *that* dirty!" Piper shivers at the thought. "Just thinkin' about it makes me wanna take a shower."

"Pipe, really? All these years in Grassy Pond, and you're still afraid of a little dirt."

I glance at Cash and know that he's thinking something. He grins before speaking.

"Too bad you pay too much for those mud facials. You could easily go to the mud hole and save yourself a ton of money."

"Cash, you have no idea what you're talking about." She gets up and takes her plate to the sink and comes back to the table. "So, what are we gonna do now?"

Cash takes our plates to the sink and turns around. I know he's already got his wheels turning in his brain. How can he say enough without raising questions from my mama?

61

"Y'all wanna ride into town with me? I heard they're having a big sale on boots at the General Store. I need a new pair of Justin's."

"Sounds good to me," I say. Piper, Tessa, and I tell Mama bye and make our way to Cash's truck. As soon as the truck is put into reverse, Piper is on us like gum stuck to the bottom of a shoe.

"What the hell is goin' on?" she asks quizzically. "I was seriously about to lose my shit in there. You had me in there with your mama, knowing I was dying to know what the hell is really goin' on."

Tessa's head does a snap from looking out the passenger side window to staring me in the eyes. "Char, spill it now before I jump over this seat and smack it outta ya!"

Dang, Tessa's in a pissy mood. I look at Cash and decide to just put it out there.

"Aight, Joe's not who he says he is. In fact, I had a bunch of crazy shit happen at school. He saw me come apart and made me feel like he was on my team, but instead, he's playing for Team Dylan."

"That fucker! I'm gonna kill him. Char, why didn't you tell me?" Tessa says as she clenches her fists.

"Because look at you. You're about to go ape shit on him. But, something is off. I know it. As soon as Joe confessed to being the one behind everything, Dylan texted me. Don't worry; I'm done keeping quiet. I'm ready to take Dylan down. Now, I just need y'all's help."

Piper hasn't said a word, and like a ton of bricks, I realize what's going on. Joe. She really likes him. I didn't even put her feelings into play when I opened my mouth. What an awful friend I am!

"Piper, I'm so sorry. I shouldn't have said it like that."

I see a glisten in her eyes, and she quickly brushes away a single tear. "No, thanks for telling the truth. But Char, I never saw that coming. He seems to have so much heart. I just talked to him yesterday. He seemed distant when I asked about you, but I just figured it had a lot to do with his parents. They are complete asshats. He's got a lot of shit going on back home." She takes a moment, and I know there is more. "Gosh, y'all, when I looked into those make-you-wanna-melt eyes, I didn't just see crystal blue, a smokin' hot body, and a one-night stand. I saw a guy with a heart of gold. He stole my heart within minutes of contact. Even if he's who you say he is, I just have to believe there's something we don't know."

Quiet tears begin to roll down Piper's face. In the seven years I've known her, I've never seen her this upset over a guy. She always knew there were more guys out there and told me to toss 'em back if the catch wasn't what I wanted. Too bad the one catch I wanted to belly-up kept returning to make my life hell. It's time for Dylan to go down.

The remainder of the drive to the General Store is pretty quiet except for the tunes coming through the speakers.

We find a parking spot on Main Street, and I decide it's time to make a statement before we check out what's on sale.

"Y'all, before we go in, I've got somethin' to say." Everyone sits still and turns toward me. Cash stretches out his hand and laces his fingers through mine. "I've made a decision. I'm going to take Dylan down... my way. I'm not exactly sure of my entire plan right now, but I know I'm going to need your help. Are y'all in?"

"It's about damn time!" Tessa states and Piper is an *Amen* right behind her. Well, with that out in the open, it's time to do a little shopping. Maybe I'll just browse because I broke the bank at Lebo's on Friday. We hop out of the truck and make our way inside. Cash drapes his arm around my shoulder and holds me close.

Chapter 9

We walk inside the General Store, and it's obvious a new stock of Rock and Roll Cowgirl apparel has arrived. Tessa and I look at each other and grin from ear to ear. *Thank goodness for Dad's credit account at the store.* We peruse the aisles, and I spot top after top after top that I'd love to have in my closet, but at fifty bucks a pop, I know it's not happening. I decide on a new gold and lace sequined top. It will look fantastic with my new boots. Tessa has two shirts, and Piper even has one. Cash, on the other hand, walks around with a box of Justin boots. I can't wait to see what they look like!

"Cash, let me see 'em." I remove the box from his arms. "Nice," I say as I enthusiastically open it. Inside is a pair of beautiful brown Bent Rail boots. They look a little worn in color. It's like when your tan begins to fade from the summer.

"So, they're keepers?" Cash questions.

"Heck, yeah! Oh, but my new ones are H-O-T! I guess I'll wear them to the McCracken's farm tonight."

We finish at the store and make our way back to the farm. On the way there, we decide what time we're meeting up tonight and discuss enjoying ourselves. The plan to take Dylan down will begin tomorrow. Here's to one more night of normalcy, I hope.

Piper heads home to get ready, Tessa goes inside, and Cash and I park it on the front porch swing.

"Char-coal, do you think he'll be there tonight? Because if he is, we need some idea of a plan. We can't get blind-sided."

"True. I told him I'd be at GPAC when I texted him back. So, I know that's where he will plan to see me. Cash, I know you're not gonna like the plan that I have playing out in my head, but it's the only way."

"What are you talkin' about, Char? Tell me now. I'm not waiting until tomorrow."

I take a calming breath before I say words that Cash is going to hate.

"Aight, since I have to go to the GPAC to stay in shape for the season, I figured I'd try to get back with Dylan." Cash cuts me off, and I can see the veins popping out of his neck because of his anger.

"Like hell you will, Charley Anne Rice! You aren't getting near him. I won't let you. You aren't puttin' yourself in danger again."

"Listen, Cash Money. I've been in danger since that god awful night. This can't be any worse because I'm gonna be the one in control. He's gonna think I'm on his team. I'll make him think I can't live without him, and just when he thinks he's got me for good, I'm gonna turn the tables and take him down. He won't hurt me or any other girl for that matter."

"I don't like this one bit, Char-coal. In fact, I want to get my rifle and blow his damn head off. You don't deserve to put yourself through this again. Just so you know, if you go through with this plan, I'm gonna be in the shadows. Always."

"Cash, I gotta do something. If he wants control, then I'm gonna make him think he has it. You better be in the shadows, but tonight, I just want a night without Dylan,

Joe, and every other piece of drama I've been dealing with lately. I want Piper, Tessa, you, and me to be like old times. My only thing is…if he shows up, the plan might have to be put into action sooner."

"Char-coal, if I have you for one night, then he's not gonna ruin it. I'm gonna make sure this is the best night of your life."

I lock my arm through his and place my head onto his shoulder as we swing on the porch swing in silence.

"Char, you better get ready if we're going to the Burger Shak," Cash says as he moves a strand of hair from my forehead.

"How long have I been knocked out?"

"Um, about thirty minutes."

"Why did you let me do that?"

"Char-coal, you are like my piece of heaven here on Earth. I couldn't stand to wake up my beautiful angel. You looked so peaceful and sweet."

At that moment, Cash Money completely stole my heart. I have no doubt that he is in my future. But, will our future survive Dylan and his control?

I look up into his eyes and just smile because there are no words to express what I am feeling inside. I love him with my every fiber of my body. He will always be my Cash Money.

"Why are you grinnin' like an opossum?" he asks as he starts to stand.

"Uh, ya know, sometimes there aren't words, Cash Money." He grabs for my hand and pulls me up into a tight bear hug. It's the type of hug that removes all air from your lungs. He releases me and begins to head toward his truck.

"I'll see ya in a lil while, Char-coal."

I stand there in complete awe as that fine ass walks to the truck. Damn. Before my brain registers with my feet, I'm less than an inch from Cash when he turns around. I wrap my arms around his neck and pull him in for a kiss that has been brewing within my soul since I understood he was always going to be my Cash Money. Forever. Time stands still. He picks me up and sits me on the tailgate without separating our lips. I want him to know that he's it. Cash is the one. The one that my heart desires for eternity. He's what makes this Char-coal feel like a diamond. He begins to control our kiss and slows it down to a smooth and steady rhythm before ending it with his head pressed against my forehead.

Catching his breath, he asks, "Char-coal, what was that? I can't let you keep pulling at my heart strings like that." I stop him from talking by placing my fingers gently over his lips.

"Cash Money, I don't know what tonight, tomorrow, or our future brings, but I want you to know that you are the one I want." His eyes get wide, and his smile grows from ear to ear. "Cash Money, I chose you, and if things don't turn out the way I hope with Dylan, I want you to know that you are my number one. You have been since we were four years old. No one will ever be able to hold my heart like you. Please remember that as the shit with Dylan plays out because I'm good at putting on the dog when needed. Just know that I'm doing this for us."

His eyes glass over, and I crash my lips back onto his. If I thought I felt hunger and desire before, I had no idea. Cash gently slides his hand behind my neck, and we savor every moment until I hear a truck coming up the drive. There's no need to act surprised. As usual, it's Dad, raining on the Cash and Charley parade. We both giggle as we break apart, and Cash gets into the truck. I walk back to the house with a smile on my face that will not quit. I love Cash Money. There, I said it, I meant it, and I want the damn T-shirt.

I meet my dad as I get to the porch steps. He's sweaty and covered in dirt from working on the fence posts all afternoon.

"Char, it's about damn time, sweetheart."

I glance at him. Did he really just say that?

"Honey, since the moment I saw you two together, I knew that you were each other's happily ever after. I just didn't know how long it would take for you to figure it out."

We make our way into the house, and I get an earful from Mama and Tessa about the show they just got in the front yard. Tessa had to be Tessa and give me a play-by-play. *Like I wasn't there!* She did it no justice whatsoever. Tessa and I tell Mama and Dad our plans for the night, and then it's time to get ready. I'm ready for a night with my sister, best friend, and the love of my life in a field with big trucks and country music. It doesn't get any better than that, and I plan to make it a night none of us forget!

Chapter 10

Taking two stairs at a time, I make my way to my bedroom. Time for a quick shower before my one night of forgetting everything begins.

Walking to my closet, I turn around and grab my bag from school. No need to think about what I'm wearing tonight. That new outfit from Lebo's is all I need. I love the gold sequined shirt I got today, but it's not really 'getting down on the farm' type attire, but that pearl snap is a different story. And, Cash is gonna love it.

Cranking up the radio, I finish getting ready. I'm almost done when Tessa bursts through the door, looking like she's on a mission for who knows what.

"Dang, Char, are you tryin' to put a hurtin' on Cash? He's not gonna let you outta this house."

"He'll let me out, but he might not let me outta his sight though," I respond as I go back to finishing my mascara.

"There's the confidence I've missed in my favorite sis."

"That's so wrong because I'm your only sister."

"I know, but it's true. Are you 'bout ready? Piper and Cash should be here any moment."

"Yup." I glide on my lipstick, pop my lips and look one more time into the mirror. I'm ready.

We walk halfway down the stairs and are met by Piper. "Dang, Char! I thought we were just going to the McCracken's?"

"What? It's my new outfit from Lebo's. You like?"

"Def your style, Char, and Cash is gonna go nuts! You're gonna drive him crazy, especially since you are trying to be Miss Independent."

Oh gosh, I know Tessa is about to give that play-by-play again. Before I can intercept her, she's spilling it to Piper loud and proud. When she finishes her version of events, we make our way down the steps, and Piper waits for my version.

"Pipe, I can't tell you right now." I point toward Mama and Dad. "I'll fill you in later, but it was a lot sweeter and not anything like that!"

The front door creaks open, and there he stands. My knight in an F250 and tonight a pair of Rock and Roll Cowboy jeans matched with a black and turquoise plaid poplin shirt. *OMG, I think I can pick my mouth off the floor right now.*

Cash closes the door and waves to my parents on his way to meet us.

"Ladies, are y'all ready?" he asks with a nod and a smile. I think I might have just melted into a puddle on the floor!

Quickly, I pull myself together, and we walk to the truck. We climb into the cab and head to the Burger Shak. *My mouth is watering already!* We sit, order, and eat with no issues like the last time. In fact, I'm totally prepared when Dustin walks in, especially when he sits beside Tessa and pulls her in for a quick kiss. My mind begins to wonder, and I feel Cash's hand squeeze my thigh. Looking at him, I can sense he's trying to reassure me that everything is okay. Then, he just puts it out there on the table.

"Dustin, do you know if Dylan is gonna be at the party tonight?"

"Nah, he's still at school. Their coach made extra practices through the weekend. I don't think he'll be home until mid-week, but when he's on his way, Charley will be the first to know. I can't believe that asshole's my damn brother."

"It's not your fault, Dustin," I say. "What are you up to tomorrow?"

"Nothin,' I don't think. Why?"

"It's time to put an end to all of this, and we need your help to do it. You in?"

"As much as I want to help, I can't really be involved. He's already suspicious of my relationship with Tessa, even though there's nothing fake about it." He pulls Tessa tighter and assures her of the truth.

"I understand, Dustin. Just be ready because I'm done playin' nice."

We finish our supper and then make our way back to Cash's truck. It's no shocker when Tessa decides to take off with Dustin and meet us there. I'm gonna have to talk to that girl. She better be using her head because I can tell she's head over heels in love with him.

Cash cranks up the truck and asks Piper if we need to find Old Man Bill to buy her some beer. And, of course, she already has it covered. Go figure.

Cash puts it in drive and heads out of town and toward the McCracken's farm. We turn up the radio to a little Cole Swindell's "Chillin' It" and sing at the top of our lungs. Cash makes quick glances at me, letting me know exactly how he feels about me.

We make our way up the dirt road with the four-wheel drive and park in the field. The bonfire is the first thing we see as the flames tower high in the sky.

Cash parks the truck and hurries around to open my door before I can hop out. Now, this is what being a gentleman is all about.

The cool, crisp air on my cheeks and the smell of burning wood heighten my senses as we make our way toward the middle of the field. Cash locks his fingers in mine as we make our way up the hill into the field. I steal a glance in his direction, and he catches me. Those eyes and that damn smile get me every time.

Piper, Cash and I hang out by the fire, and Piper pops a top out of her purse. *How does she fit all that shit in there?* She offers me a beer, and I shake my head no. These memories don't need any clouds in the way. As if Cash knows what I'm thinking, he produces a Choice Cherry Gold. I twist off the cap and take in the sweet cherry goodness. A Choice Cherry Gold, a roaring fire, country music blaring, and my two best friends by my side. It doesn't get any better than this.

Piper spots Justin making his way up the hill. No matter how long we're gone from Grassy Pond, when we return, it's like time has stood still, and we pick up where we left off. Piper opens a new beer and saunters her cute self toward Justin. Like I said, it's like we never left. Justin looks hot as always with his two brothers on each

73

side of him and a Coleman cooler in his hand. Cash stands behind me and pulls me into him as we watch Piper walk away. She's got him wrapped around her little finger. Cash wraps his arms around me, and I glance over my shoulder to look at that perfectly chiseled face.

"You know, Char-coal, he ain't ever gonna get over her." I close my eyes, pull his arms tighter, and savor every moment I have with Cash Money. Just like I'll never get over Cash Money.

As the music begins to slow, I realize it's Eli Young Band's "Crazy Girl". How fitting. Cash's arms tighten, and we begin to sway back and forth as he whispers into my ear the lyrics, "Have I told you lately I love you like crazy, girl?" Every ounce of control and desire unite at once. I turn and face Cash and put my forehead against his as he sings the entire song to me. I don't close my eyes; I look deep into the soul of my childhood love. It's evident that this isn't a childhood crush. He's the love of my life that's willing to let me live my life and come back to him when I'm ready. Unfortunately, it all comes down to Dylan. Will I be able to escape his control and will my plan play out like I wish? The song ends, and Cash's lips graze mine with soft, tender warmth. I feel my temperature rise because I cannot get enough of Cash Money.

I realize we now have an audience and think that might not be the best game plan for what I have in mind for the remainder of my break.

"Cash Money, I don't wanna stop, but if we want to make the plan work, then we need to make it look like we're not together… and this… makes us look like we're together."

Cash takes a minute to distance himself from me. I hate the fact that we are going to have to play enemies for the next month or so, but it has to be done.

I move in close to him again. "Just remember the club. It's our place. It will always be, and we can always be ourselves there."

"Well then, Char-coal, you better plan on camping out tonight."

"You got it."

Tessa and Dustin arrive ten minutes later. I inwardly question what my sister's been up to because she looks like she's been up to no good! They approach us, and she gives me the look like don't even say what you're thinking. I don't say a word right now, but I will later. That's what big sisters are for, right?

We spend the rest of the night catching up with old friends. Justin and Piper are in their own little world while Tessa, Dustin, Cash, and I hang out, laughing at all the drunken country folk.

Around midnight, I'm beat and ready to call it a night. I break up Justin and Piper's tonsil hockey session and tell her this chick is leaving. She just grins because I know she's leaving with Justin. We give Tessa and Dustin a little privacy while they say their goodbyes, but don't think I don't holler for her to hurry it up. She shoots me the bird and then makes her way to the truck.

"Char, are you freakin' kidding me? I mean, damn! Can't I get a break?"

"Hey, Dustin could have taken you home, but I doubt Dad would want you rolling in this late with him. Oh, and what took y'all so long tonight? Was that like the dessert from earlier?"

"What if it was?" Tessa smirks.

"You better be using your head. That's what I'm sayin'."

"So, where are we meeting tomorrow to put this plan into action?" Cash says, breaking the tension between Tessa and me.

"The club at three o'clock?" I reply.

"Sounds good to me," Tessa answers, and Cash nods.

"Hey, Tessa, will you let Dustin know? I'll text Piper."

"Sure."

We make our way back to the farm, and Cash pulls into the driveway. Tessa jumps out first, and I go to open the door when Cash says my name.

"Char-coal."

I stop and turn to face him. He brings his hand to my face and brushes his thumb along my lips before pulling me in for a kiss that speaks more than words ever could. The hunger I feel for him ignites, and I can't get close enough to him.

Before I have time to think about what I'm doing, I'm straddling Cash in the driver's seat of his truck. The kiss is no longer sweet and innocent, but fuel to a fire that has been burning for over a decade. My hands run up his washboard stomach, and his hands squeeze my thighs like he is trying to gain control of the emotions that he has lost. I don't want him to; I want him to let go of those emotions because tonight could be the last night I get to stay with him as just Char-coal and Cash Money. Tomorrow, I put up a new front, one that says I want Dylan Sloan back in my life. It is a front that is the biggest pile of horse shit I have ever heard.

Cash begins to slow down and brushes my hair from my face. He breaks our kiss and looks into my soul. He doesn't have to say what he's thinking because I know. I know he loves me for me. Plain ol' Char-coal.

"Char-coal, we've got to stop. If we keep going at this rate, I'm not going to be able to stop myself, and when I'm finally with you, it's gonna be special. The two of us in the front seat of the truck ain't special. You deserve better than that." He kisses my lips. "Now, are we going to the club or what?"

"Damn straight, we are. I'll meet you there in fifteen." I slide to the passenger seat, grab my purse, and make my way to the house.

Before going inside, I glance over my shoulder and wave to Cash. Trying to calm my emotions, I take a few deep breaths and go inside. Of course, Mama and Dad are waiting up, even though they are asleep on the couch. They are too cute.

I walk over to them and give them a nudge to tell them we're home. They claim they had just closed their eyes and weren't sleeping. *Whatever!* I let them know I need to go to the club. My mama gives me a look that I've never seen before, and then she says what I thought I'd never hear.

"Char, are you sure that's the best idea? I mean, we trust you two completely, but don't put yourself in a situation that leaves open doors for mistakes to be made."

"Mama! Are you kidding me? It's Cash for crying out loud!"

"That's exactly my point. You love him with your heart, and he feels the same way. Things can happen, ya know?"

"Stop, Mama! It won't. I'm going." I turn around and hear my dad in the background. He can't believe she just said that, but I bet he actually can.

I hustle up the steps, change into a pair of black yoga pants, tank, and a Southern swimming hoodie. I slide on my boots, tell Tessa I'll see her in the morning and grab stuff for PB&J sandwiches, chips, and two Choice Cherry Golds. I make my way to the barn, crank up the four-wheeler and head to the club. I'm not surprised to see the light is already on.

Once I get to the club, I toss my stuff over my shoulder and climb up the ladder. I place my bag onto the floor before climbing inside. I turn around to see Cash Money, standing in a pair of loose-fitting Under Armour fleece pants, long-sleeved T-shirt, and ball cap. *Damn. Mama might have been right.* He squats down to adjust the heater and then looks up at me.

"You brought PB&J's? Sweet."

He turns on the radio, and we sit in the floor and make sandwiches. Just like it's us against the world, Cash and I fall into our own bubble.

After our midnight snack, Cash cleans up the mess because we sure don't want any unwanted critters tonight. When he finishes, he steals my heart with a Hershey's bar, marshmallows, and graham crackers. There's nothing like S'mores over a kerosene heater.

We sit in front of the heater and make a S'more each. When I catch my marshmallow on fire, Cash quickly blows out the flame and pulls it off the hanger and eats it.

"Hey! That was mine!"

He shrugs his shoulder as he smirks and chews the marshmallow like it's the best thing he's ever eaten. Two can play this game. Taking another marshmallow, I toast it perfectly and remove it from my hanger, getting the ooey gooey goodness on my fingers. I place it into my mouth, chew, and then lick my fingers a little too seductively. Cash stops mid-bite of his S'more, and his mouth hits the floor.

"Remember, Cash. I always win," I say with confidence.

"Char-coal, you're always number one in my book, and right now I'm going to kiss you."

Cash puts down his S'more, takes my hanger from my hands, and closes the space between us. We are now face-to-face. His hardworking hands enclose my face, and I can feel the rough calluses from the hours he's spent working on the farm. If a guy can do that much with his hands on the farm, Lord knows what else he can do with them.

I close my eyes and get lost in my senses, smelling the open country, heater, chocolate, and Cash's never-changing perfect scent. His lips brush mine in slow pecks, but then turn into a long, passionate war within our souls. The tug-of-war that we have been playing for so many years is now at the surface, and it is no longer being hidden like a flame in the night.

Cash and I get lost in each other, but he remains in control. If I had something to do with it, I would have given him all of me right there on the floor in the club. Cash distances himself when things get too intense, but the struggle is obvious. He reminds me that he wants me to be treated like a queen. He pulls me into his arms, and we enjoy each other.

As soon as I begin to yawn, he leads me by the hand to the futon and covers me while he starts a movie. I snicker when I see what movie he has with him. *Sweet Home Alabama.*

"Awe, Cash, you love this movie as much as I do, huh?"

"Maybe."

"Hey, Cash Money, what's your favorite part?"

He hits *Play* and lies on the futon beside me. "Definitely when she realizes she gave away her heart a long time ago and the fact that the country boy beats the city slicker hands down."

"I love you. You know that, right? Now, no talking for the next one hundred and nine minutes."

"You got it, Char-coal." He kisses the top of my head, and we don't say another word until the movie is over.

"Why is it when you've seen a movie a hundred times, you still watch it from start to finish, no matter how tired you are?" I ask.

"I guess it's kinda like this, Char-coal. I could watch you from now until we're no longer on this Earth, and it wouldn't be enough. Sometimes you know a good thing when you see it."

I roll over and look at him. "I think you just stole my heart, again. I love you, Cash Money. I need you to remember that. I need you to be sure of that when things don't look that way starting tomorrow." I take his face in my hands. "Do you, Cash? Promise me that when this is over, it's you and me. No matter what I have to do to get there. Don't let what I do with Dylan interfere with us. Promise me."

"I promise you, Char-coal. You already have my heart and soul and that will not change. I love you."

Our lips crash into each other as the tears fall from my eyes. I have just given away my heart, and tomorrow I'm making a pact with the devil.

Eventually, our lips slow, and we drift off to sleep. We wake to the sounds of the wind whipping around the club.

The sun peeks through the window, and I pull the cover over my head. "Do we have to get up?" I mumble to Cash. He doesn't answer; he just wraps his arm tighter around me and kisses my neck.

We embrace the cold air and make our way back to our separate farms. Within a few hours, our world will be different.

I hurry home, shower, eat a fabulous breakfast from my mama, including bacon, of course, and then get ready for church.

Cash sits on the pew behind me, and my heart warms just knowing he is close to me. Tessa looks like a lost puppy without Dustin by her side. It's kinda sweet to see her actually fall for someone. I just hope Dustin doesn't have an ounce of Dylan in him, because if he hurts her, I'll kill him. Oh goodness, I'm making threats in my mind at church! *Get out! Get out! Get out!* I tell myself.

I push those thoughts from my mind and focus on the choir and sermon. I leave church with a peaceful and easy feeling that everything will be okay.

After Sunday lunch, Tessa and I decide to relax until time to meet at the club. As we watch *CMT*, I get a text from Piper.

Piper: I'll be there in 20

Me: k

When *CMT Top 20* comes on, Tessa and I rock out in the living room. Piper sneaks inside the house, and we realize that she's videoed the entire thing.

"Pipe, that better not get put on any website. You got that?"

"Now, why would I do that to y'all?"

I look at Tessa, and she reads my mind. One. Two. Three. We run straight for her and her phone. That is so getting deleted.

After what feels like a tug-of-war, Tessa manages to grab the phone. She hits *Delete*, and then her face looks like she's seen a ghost.

"Tessa, what's wrong?" She doesn't answer. "*Tessa?*"

"You bitch! How could you still talk to him?"

Wait. Talk to whom? The world is spinning out of control as I see Tessa moving toward Piper. She's gonna beat her ass. I can see it in her eyes.

"Both of you stop!" I scream. "What's going on?"

"Char, she's still talking to Joe! Can you believe that? Look right here." Tessa points to Piper's text messages. A piece of my heart just broke, and I feel like I'm going to puke.

I look at Piper, but the words don't come.

"Char, I'm sorry. He needed someone to talk to. I feel like there is something we don't know. I just couldn't let him do this alone."

"Alone? Piper! I've been alone for how long? He needs to suffer for what he did to me! He lied! He watched me give a piece of my soul to him, and he still couldn't confess until he was completely shitfaced!"

About this time, my mama walks into the room to see if everything is okay. Over the years, she has learned that the three of us are like sisters and are better off to just duke it out and then we are good. The question I will now have to deal with is, what did she hear?

"Charley Anne, I think it's time you start talking. I know there is something going on, and I have for a while. Spill it."

The lump in my throat is full and tight. "Mama, it's nothing, okay. Piper's been talking to Joe, and he's an ass. That's all."

"Young lady, watch your mouth. I'm sure Piper has a good explanation for this, but I will not have all this yelling going on. Get yourselves together."

I can still feel the flames coming out of my ears, so I try to calm myself. Piper, Tessa, and I look at each other. This conversation is far from over. We put on a happy face, tell Mama bye, and make our way to the club because out there she can't hear us.

Chapter 11

No words are spoken as we walk to the Gator inside the barn. I get into the driver's seat, and we make our way to the club. I take out my emotions with speed. The faster, the better.

We park and stand there in silence.

"What the hell, Piper? You're my best friend! Can't you put your damn feelings for a guy to the side for once? For me at least?"

"Oh! Me! Charley, you just keep whatever guy you want at the time close by. You're just mad because he actually likes me for me. You're jealous."

"Jealous, my ass! He lied to me! He's Team Dylan, or did you forget about the moment in hell I experienced?"

"Char, I couldn't forget what happened to you if I tried, but I know that there's more to this than Joe's saying. Something bad happened to him, too! I think Dylan has it out for him as well. I couldn't just walk out of his life. That has happened to him too many times. I love him, Char. I really love him!"

"But yet, you left with Justin last night. Oh, that's smart!"

"Hold up, you two! You've been friends too long to let some boy ruin it. Both of your emotions are crazy right now. Don't say something you're gonna regret later. I'll tell you this, Piper, you better not get too close to him until you know the truth," Tessa states.

With that comment, I hear Cash's four-wheeler approaching. When he pulls up, we get quiet. I'm sure it's obvious something is going on.

"Um, did I miss a cat fight?" Cash laughs.

"I guess you could say that," Tessa says smartly.

We make our way up the club ladder and into the club. We grab a drink from the fridge, and then I let my thoughts spill from my mouth.

"I'm tired. I'm tired of Dylan scaring the hell out of me. I'm tired of Joe lying to me, tired of not being able to be with Cash like I want, and tired of life in general. This is supposed to be a fun time in my life, yet Dylan is always in the picture somehow. So, I'm going back to him."

Cash winces at the words, Tessa starts to argue with me, and Piper looks like she wants to slap me.

"No, listen to me. He thinks he has control over me. Yes, he's scared me, broke Joe's trust, kept tabs on me, but he hasn't stopped me from enjoying the one thing he thought he took away from me completely." They stare at me like they are lost. "Swimming. When he texted me after the Joe incident, I made sure to mention I'd see him at GPAC. He didn't reply. That shows that he knows that he's starting to lose his hold. I plan to see him at the pool during the break and fall for him again. Then, I'll take his ass down in the water and with the court system if I have to. I can't let him hurt another girl like he did me. If I keep quiet, then he'll do it again. But, why me? That part I still don't understand." In the mist of my rambling, Cash decides to enlighten us.

"If y'all don't mind, can I give you a guy's perspective?" We all look at each other and nod. "I'm not saying that I understand Dylan because I'd never do that to anyone, ever. I do understand the whole male territory thing. Charley, when y'all started dating, it took everything I had in me not to act like a freakin' caveman. I wanted to claim you as mine. Then when he... he... raped you, I thought I was going to kill him. He staked his claim in the worst way possible. The fact that we're the only ones that know means that he still has the upper hand. Once we tell, he's going to give in. He will completely lie about it and try to act like it was all you."

"See, that's where this plan gets interesting. I'm not just gonna run to the cops. I'm going to start dating him again."

"Like hell you are, Charley!" Tessa yells.

"Yes. I. Am. If I can get him to trust me, then maybe I can get him to admit it to me. Why? I need to know why, and I hope to have a recording of him saying it."

Piper and Tessa begin to have their own conversation about why this isn't a good idea, but Cash pulls them back to the reality of the situation and why it has to be this way.

"Girls, if Char can get Dylan to admit it and we have proof, then the ball's in her court. It will bring down Dylan Sloan. I'm sure of it. Plus, do y'all really think that she's going to get that close to him without me nearby?"

"So, how do we play into this?" Piper asks.

"I just need you to know the truth. No matter what happens, you know I love Cash. You know that this has to happen. We have to make it look believable, especially with my parents. My mama's already planning my wedding to Cash, so I'm sure I'm going to have a lot of questions to answer." Cash's head spins around like I've said something crazy. "Don't act like you didn't know that," I say.

"Well, it's one thing to know it and another to say it out loud," he says. I swear his eyes are about to bug outta his head.

"Are y'all ready for how this is really gonna go down?"

"Well, we don't have much of a choice, do we?" Piper says to Tessa.

"Aight, I'm starting practice tomorrow morning. Coach has sent our winter break workouts to the head of the aquatic centers. I have to train a minimum of four days a week. Guess who else has to as well? Dylan. I'm going to have two days on him and my routine. I'm going to act like he doesn't exist, and I know him well enough to know that will drive him crazy. Hell, that's what got me into this mess to start with. I didn't give him the time of day. Let's see how long it takes for him to try working his charm again. If he doesn't, then I'm going to make him want me. I'm gonna stop at nothing to make this happen. That's why I keep telling y'all who I really love. 'Cause appearances are going to look otherwise. Once I go back to school, I'm gonna use the Kluft girls to keep my focus to appear that I'm head over heels in love with Dylan. Then, at Southern States, he's going down. I'm gonna make him famous just like Kelleigh Bannen's song."

For about a minute, no one says a word.

"Char, I see one problem." I look at Piper like what could she know that I don't. "Joe. He knows the truth, and he ain't gonna believe this for shit!"

The sound of his name makes my blood boil for the second time today, but she is right.

"Piper, as much as I hate to admit I'm wrong, you are definitely right." I'm trying to find the right words because I'm about to give her what she wants to hear. "I guess you're going to have to fix that, huh?"

"Does everyone hear that? Charley Anne just told us she doesn't know everything. I think the world might have stopped! You're giving me permission to talk to Joe. I have witnesses."

She looks around, and I roll my eyes. "Yes, that is what I'm saying, but don't get caught up in his lies, Piper. I really want to believe him, but I've been burned one too many times."

"What do Dustin and I need to do?" Tessa questions.

"You need to be the ears in the Sloan house. Know what's going on. I don't know if Dustin will be able to help. I know it has to be hard being his brother and all, but I know he doesn't want someone else to get hurt. Tessa, you by my side in that house will make this story believable. You've gotta be the glue that holds all my broken pieces together."

"Gotcha covered, Sis. Oh, and one more thing, how are we gonna communicate? You know he's gonna check your phone."

"Easy. Tessa and Piper won't look curious, and Cash won't either. 'Cause remember when this really happened? Cash continued to be Cash until I told him to leave me alone. We need to keep that up."

"Okay, Char-coal, but what if I really need to talk to you?" Cash asks.

I smile from ear to ear. "Cash Money, do you remember what you bought me for my ninth birthday?"

He nods his head and grins. "Walkie-talkies."

"Exactly, and you know they still work, right? So, I'll radio you as soon as I get home, and if you need me, just text Tessa."

"Char, that's all fine and dandy, but what if this plan is in full force? You can't carry a walkie-talkie the size of Texas around in your pocketbook."

"I guess I haven't thought that through. Um...Y'all know anything about those prepaid phones?"

"Not really, but I mean, it can't be that hard to get one. Heck, I know I have an old phone at the house. It's not fancy or anything. Let's just see about adding minutes to it. That way we can keep in touch," Piper says. "Charley, you'll just have to make sure Dylan doesn't see it, or you are done for. I'll check on that tomorrow morning."

"Thanks, Piper. I'm sorry about before. I mean, I don't understand you and Joe, but it's not my place to say who you love."

"Love? What the hell did I miss?" Cash ask.

Piper, Tessa, and I laugh like little girls, and Cash is completely clueless. Walking over to him, I pat him on the back and then whisper into his ear, "You know how I feel about you?" He nods. "Yeah, Piper kinda feels that way about Joe, and Tessa was gonna whoop her ass."

"I sure do wish I'd been a fly on the wall! So, I was right when I said I missed a cat fight? Damn my timing."

We spent what felt like hours discussing the ins and outs of the plan, unsure of the outcome, but knowing it had to be done. As the afternoon begins to vanish in the skyline, I look at Cash and he knows exactly what I'm thinking. It's a good thing hunting is legal on Sundays. I'm gonna find a tree.

Piper and Tessa make their way back to the house on the Gator, and I ride with Cash on the back of his four-wheeler to the barn. I grab my jacket, toboggan, coveralls, and gun from the safe, and then we return to the club. Today, we are hunting straight out the window.

We sit there quietly for over an hour before we see a little doe walk out from the east. Ten minutes later, we notice two more and a young buck. I look at Cash, and he's thinking like me. Let's let him walk and save him for next year.

We decide that we aren't pulling the trigger this evening. This is our way of coping with the cards that are currently on the table. Cash, the club, a rifle, Mother Nature, and I. I know that when I wake up tomorrow morning this won't be happening for who knows how long. I'm savoring this moment until I have to act like I'm Team Dylan Sloan.

The sky turns dark, and I know that it's time to head home. I look at Cash, and he realizes it, too.

Standing, I look into his eyes, and the water begins to build.

"Don't do this, Char-coal. He won't be here until Wednesday, so we have until then, okay?"

I nod, and the tears roll. "But, I have to pull away. If I don't, no one is going to believe it. I don't know if I can play two sides. I love you with every ounce of my being. I can't even think about what I might have to do with Dylan to get him to admit what he did and the person he is."

Cash lifts my chin, so our eyes meet. "Listen, Char-coal. You do not have to do anything with him. Do you understand? The moment that line gets crossed is the moment I step in. He will not hurt you. The next person to have you will be me on our wedding night. That is a promise I plan to keep. Well, that is if you see it in your future."

Cash looks unsure of himself, so I gaze into his eyes and bring him back to reality with my favorite movie line of all time. "Cash Money, what you wanna marry me for anyways?"

He gives me a crooked little grin and replies, "So, I can kiss you anytime I want." And with that quote, our fate is sealed with a kiss.

Chapter 12

Cash drives me back to the house on his four-wheeler. During the entire ride, I hold onto him like my life depends on it. Closing my eyes, I take in all that is around me. I want to take this moment and freeze it in time.

As the four-wheeler begins to slow, I know that it's time to put the plan into action. Cash can't go into the house. I have to give my parents motive to believe that I don't want him. But, how? I motion for Cash to go toward the barn before we get to the house.

Cash pulls up to the rear side of the barn and leaves the motor running while he waits for me to speak, but the words won't come out. I reach around him and turn off the ignition, then I wrap my arms around his waist and don't let go.

"Char-coal, please don't make this any harder than it's going to be." I loosen my grip, even though I don't want to. He steps off the four-wheeler and begins to pace back and forth. "I don't think I can let you do this, Char. I mean, I know I have to 'cause you're going to regardless, but the thought of him near you is making me insane and this plan hasn't even begun yet. How do you think I'm going to be once Dylan is home and in the picture for real?"

I sit on the four-wheeler unable to move, speak, react, or anything. Cash is telling the truth. I haven't even put myself in his shoes. Hell, I think that's what's got us into the situation in the first place. I've got to do something before Cash spins out of control before things start.

I swing my right leg over the four-wheel and scoot off. Cash has finally quit pacing and is now staring into the moonlight over the field. I grab him by his arm and pull him with all my might against the side of the barn. He looks at me like I've lost my damn mind.

"Cash, this is for us. You and me, remember? You and me." Each time I say those words I press my lips into his. "You and me." I swear I see tears begin to form in his eyes.

"I just love you so damn much. It's tearing' me up just playing' out all these scenarios that could happen in my brain."

"Listen, Cash Money. I choose you, and we have been together forever. You know me better than myself. You will know when no one else does what I'm really feeling. I promise you this. When I know that I have Dylan where I want him, I will not leave you in the dark. In fact, I want you by my side when he gets brought back to the reality that I'm in control of my life."

"Char, here's my problem. Now that I know you've chosen me, I'm gonna have a helluvia time not going all caveman territorial on his ass."

"We have one problem, Cash, and that's why I said to stop here. I gotta make Mama and Dad think you pissed me off royally. So, how do you suggest we do that?"

Cash doesn't say a word. Instead, he pulls me in for a long, slow kiss. I try to ask him what his plan might be in between kisses, but he just mumbles to me that he's thinking. I guess I can work with that.

After our heavy make-out session, Cash and I come to the realization that we are probably done seeing and talking to each other except from a distance for the majority of the break. Just thinking of a moment lost without him hurts my soul.

We agree the best way to say he pissed me off is that he got trigger happy and shot Bambi. It might sound crazy, but even though I love to hunt and take down *the one*, I can't stand for a baby's life to be taken too soon. So, this just might be the spark to light the kerosene. Knowing that it will need to be more than that, we decide the other half to this equation is me feeding my parents a lie that Cash doesn't want me to go back to Southern. He wants me to stay in Grassy Pond. Now, that is totally believable and enough to tick off my dad royally.

"Cash, we have to start this now, ya know?"

"Uh-huh," he says as his lips touch mine like he's savoring every moment.

"Cash, I love you, and the minute all this shit is over, it's you and me, forever. You got that?"

"And that, Char-coal, is why I'm letting you go through with this. Listen. When I drop you off at the house, you better cause one hell of a scene. I mean, I want boot stomping, spitting nails, pissed off at Cash Money like never before. Got it?"

"Damn straight, I do! Pretty much, I just act like you're the asshat known as Dylan."

"Yeah, why didn't we think of that earlier?"

"I dunno, but the sooner we start this plan, the faster it's gonna be over." He pulls me to him and turns me to where I am now backed against the wall. He kisses my lips feverishly and then picks me up as I wrap my legs around his waist. If this happens to be the last time I kiss Cash Money, I wanna make sure that neither one of us forgets. Nothing, and I mean nothing, will ever erase this perfect memory. I also don't think I'll ever look at this side of the barn the same again.

Cash places me back onto the ground, and I gain my balance. We walk hand-in-hand to the four-wheeler and make the trip to the house. Cash drives extra slowly until he knows it's time for the show to start. He cranks up the speed and guns it to the front of the house. *Here goes nothing.* I jump off the back of the four-wheeler and yell at the top of my lungs, "I hate you!" He flinches and I cower as the words spew from my mouth. I blow a kiss as I look at him one last time, then I do a one-eighty, and march my boot stompin' ass up the stairs. By the time I get to the top step, the front door is open, and my dad is giving Cash a look that might just kill him. *So far, so good.* Now, let's just see if I can pull off a good act inside.

"Charley Anne, what the hell is going on?" Dad asks.

"Dad, Cash freakin' killed Bambi! Bambi! The deer still had spots for cryin' out loud, but that's not even what matters anymore. He wants me to drop out of Southern. He wants me to stay in Grassy Pond and get married! Like now. Not wait until I graduate, and who knows, maybe even make Olympic trials! I will not stop my life for him."

My dad stands there with his hands in his pockets, looking for the right words to say. As he begins to speak, Mama starts her own rant about how she can't believe Cash would do that. That's where she played right into my hands.

"See, Mama. There you go taking his side instead of mine. I knew this was going to happen. I'm done talkin' to all of y'all." I march upstairs and slam the door for an added effect. I pull out my cell and text Cash.

Me: I made them believe Cash $

Cash: I knew u had a good poker face when you have 2

Me: I hate hurting them. U think they r goin 2 hate me when it's over?

Cash: No, they could never hate you Char-coal. I love u, and I want u to always remember that.

Me: I love u 2, and it kills me 2 know what we have 2 do 2 make this stop. I'm going to pool @8. Tessa will text u when I'm home.

Cash: k I'll be waiting. Love u Char-coal, 4ever

Me: Love u 4ever

With that response, I place my phone onto the dresser and get ready for bed. That is when my bedroom door creaks open, and Tessa is standing there with her eyes half-open.

"Um, you wanna explain all that yellin' downstairs?" she says as she crawls onto my queen-sized bed and makes herself comfortable.

"We had to make it look believable, ya know? The whole Cash and me being done story."

"Oh, so you chose this late at night for that? What did you tell Mama and Dad? I heard something about Bambi. I know that's not the bullshit line you fed them. Please tell me they have higher IQ's than that!"

"Well, I used that for starters, but then made them think he wants to get married now and me drop out of Southern."

"Char, that's good. Damn good! Oh, I'd hate to be Cash when Dad sees him tomorrow. He better hope he doesn't have a gun!"

"I know. I'm going to the pool at eight. I told Cash you'd text him after I got back. Tessa, not being able to talk to him is gonna kill me."

"You can use mine, but hey, all I'm gonna say is there will be no sexting going on here! You got that? I will not be a part of that."

"Shut up, Tess! And slide over. This is my bed, not yours!"

Tessa and I fall asleep and awake to Mama making an abundance of racket downstairs. She must be taking my drama out on a pan of biscuits, and as bad as it sounds, I can't wait to eat them!

I roll out of bed, brush my teeth, hair, and throw on my sweats before grabbing my swim bag and walking downstairs.

I decide not to sit and eat breakfast. That would mean twenty questions from Mama. I grab a biscuit, a gallon of butter, bacon and walk out the door. *Yummy.* I put the Honda in the wind and make my way to GPAC. It's now or never, and I just might be rethinking this breakfast because my nerves are about to get the best of me. To settle my uneasiness, I sing to the local country station between bites of bacon.

Pulling into the parking lot, I notice a lot of familiar cars, and even though the anxiety is about to kill me, I'm excited at the same time. I have spent most of my life here if I wasn't at school or the farm. It's my second home, and when I walked away, I left a piece of it behind. It's time to pick up that piece and begin to mend my broken heart.

I giggle to myself, noticing that *my* spot is open. The one that I've parked in since the day I got my license. I ease on in, put the car into park, take a deep breath, grab my bag, put on my game face, and walk into GPAC with confidence.

As I open the door and make my way through the check-in station, I'm attacked by a high-squealing, three-foot leg parasite, also known as Molly, Coach Stephens' daughter.

"Hey, Molly!" I rub her head, and she looks up at me. "I sure have missed you, munchkin! What have you been up to?" I ask as I pull her from my leg and pick her up.

"I learned how to write my name! And… Dad taught me how to do a backflip off the diving board. You wanna see?"

"Oh my! I have got to see that backflip! I can't believe you're in kindergarten this year! Where is your dad? I think he has something for me. You want to help me find him?" Molly nods with the excitement that only children can show.

As I put her on the ground, she grabs my hand and drags me toward Coach's office. I have a feeling he has been waiting for me.

"Slow down, munchkin." We make our way to Coach Stephens' office, and Molly knows exactly where to find him because it is pretty early for him to be coaching. Lap swim is currently in session.

Coach Stephens is looking at a new Speedo catalog. He must be getting ready to order a new stock of suits for the swim shop.

"Dad! Look who's here!" Molly exclaims, pulling Coach Stephens from his thoughts.

"Charley! How are you doing?" he says once he gets his bearings together.

"I'm doing well, Coach. I guess you heard I walked on at Southern. It feels so good to be back in the water. Did my coach email you my workouts?"

"She did. Now, what I want to know is, what changed your mind? From what I can recall, you were determined never to swim again. I know it's your business and not mine, but you are the best swimmer to ever step foot into this place."

What do I say to that? "Well, let's just say that I found some fabulous friends that googled me, and the rest is history. Oh, and Coach is super cool!"

He looks at me like he knows there has to be more, but then just proceeds to hand me the workout. He just replies with one simple comment, "It's good to have you back, Charley. This place has missed you, especially Molly."

"I've missed it, too. You know it's like a second home to me. Oh, and Molly mentioned that she can do a backflip off the diving board now. That's awesome. She's got a career in diving in her future. I'm sure of that!"

He laughs, and I leave Molly with him as I go into the locker room and get ready for workout number one of break. The aroma of warm chlorine hits my nostrils and is perfectly familiar when I walk into the pool area. I know what my permanent fragrance will be during break. It's just one of those smells that you can't get out of your skin.

I take a minute to stretch and look over the workout. It's not too bad today, but tomorrow might kill me! Dipping my cap into the water and getting ready to jump in, I notice Molly sitting on the sidelines ready to watch me. I smile and give her a wave. She is so stinkin' cute and is like the team's little cheerleader. This is all she has ever known. I slide on my cap, put my goggles in place, shake my arms to loosen them a little more, and then dive in for a 500-meter choice warm-up.

I continue through the sets listed and finish my workout in a little over an hour and a half. As I remove my cap, I arch my head backward into the water before pushing my arms up on the side of the pool and jumping out. It feels amazing to be completely in my element in the place I used to call home.

After showering and getting ready for the day ahead, I make my way back to the front to check out, but not before telling Coach Stephens and Molly bye.

Getting back into my car, I let out a sigh of relief and head back to the farm. Piper, Cash, Tessa, and I have a few kinks to work out. I send Tessa and Piper a text, and they will let Cash know.

Me: On way 2 farm

Piper: Meet u there for shopping in 1 hr

Tessa: I'm ready 2

With that text, I know shopping refers to a new phone and attitude. I also know that Tessa will let Cash know the deal, and that we will meet up at some point today. If I have to watch Cash from a distance too long, I just might go insane. That boy has my body in one tangled up hot mess!

After arriving at the farm, I try to make a beeline for my room, so I can escape the questioning from Mama just a little bit longer. That is put to a halt when she summons me to the living room as I am halfway up the stairs. Doing an about-face, I put on my best poker face and get ready to lie to my parents, something that I do not want to do.

"Yes, Mama?"

"Charley, we need to talk."

"About what?"

"You, Cash, and what you're hiding."

Hiding? Does she know? What does she think I'm hiding? My palms begin to sweat, and I try my best to hide my true feelings.

"Mama, I'm fine. Cash just pissed me off. I want to be me. No one telling me what to do, where to be, and I want to just experience life. He's trying to smother me."

"I understand that, but as your mother, I can't help but feel like there's something you're not telling me."

"That's it."

Mama gains her composure before finally saying what she is thinking.

"Charley, you know you can talk to me about anything. Did things go too far with Cash?"

I am at a loss for words. She is still stuck on that.

"Mama! I can't believe you keep thinking that! Please believe me. You know that I wouldn't do that! Seriously, what do I have to say to make you believe that we haven't crossed that line?"

"Charley, I believe you. I just feel like something isn't right from last night. I mean, you couldn't keep your hands off each other, or should I say lips, and then he suddenly goes barbaric on you. Telling you what you're going to do. Cash has never told you what to do, so I'm not buying it!?"

Mama crosses her arms and waits for my reaction and comment.

"Mama, I don't know. It's like he has totally lost it or something. Who knows? Maybe it's me. Maybe I'm the one losing it. I just love Southern, the team, my hallmates, and my life there. I'm not ready to settle down. If he's not careful, I'm gonna totally push myself from him."

"Spoken like the Charley I know. You have grown so much since you left in August, and I'm proud of you. I'm not going to say I buy all of this between you and Cash, but that's y'all's business, not mine."

This is getting too nosey and serious. Time for a change of subject.

"So…Piper, Tessa, and I are going to Northlake. Anything you want for Christmas?"

"Nah, I'm good. Just having you home is Christmas for me." Mama walks over to me and pulls me in for a hug. "I've missed you, sweet girl."

We break our embrace, and I make my way upstairs to talk to Tessa before leaving, and hopefully, talk to Cash, too. I've not even gone twenty-four hours without him, and I'm a complete mess.

I knock as I walk into Tessa's room. "Hey, Tess, I'm back. Can I call Cash?"

"Sure, but I don't know how you're gonna go through with this plan."

"Me either. Mama just gave me the third degree down there, and now we have to go to Northlake because I told her that's what we're doing."

"Nice and well played."

"I try. Now, let me see that phone." With an eye roll, Tessa gives me the phone and then excuses herself while I call Cash. He answers on the second ring.

"Hey, Tessa. Everything good?"

"It's perfect now that I'm talkin' to you," I reply in a smooth, sultry voice.

"Char-coal, I'm so glad to hear your voice. I mean, I know it's not even been a day, but it's killin' me. How was the pool?"

"Great! Molly attacked me as soon as I walked inside the center, and Coach Stephens was the same old coach. It felt great to be there. Since it was just lap swim, I didn't see any team folks. I think I'll stick with that time while I'm home."

"That's great. So, what is the plan for the rest of the day?"

"Well, just so you know, Mama totally called me out a few minutes ago about us, but I think I at least got her to quit asking questions. I hope because I can't lie to her forever."

"You do know you don't have to lie. We could come clean with everything about Dylan."

"What do you mean 'we'?"

"I just meant I'd be there with you, like I have since it happened."

"Thanks, Cash Money. If only I could kiss those sweet lips of yours right now."

"How about when y'all get back, you meet me at the club?"

"Sounds good to me. I guess I better go. I love you."

"I love you, too."

After hanging up and walking downstairs, I think about what is going on and what I'm about to do. I know it's what is needed, but to put my family, friends, and Cash through this, is it worth it? Most definitely.

Tessa and I make our way outside when we hear Piper toot the horn. We wave bye to Mama and Dad who are sitting on the porch.

After getting into the car, we both let out a sigh of relief.

"That bad, huh?" Piper says.

"Let's just say that you know how your mama number two can be."

"Awe, lawd! I'd love to have been a fly on the wall. She was houndin' ya with all those questions. I can just hear her now."

"It's not funny, Pipe. If she keeps this up, there is no way I'm gonna be able to go through with the plan."

"Easy then, Sis. Don't. Go to Mama and Dad, the police…anyone…and tell. Just tell."

"I wish it were that simple, but you know it's not. No one will believe me, and there is no evidence."

"What do you mean, 'no evidence'? Where are all the texts, pics, and Facebook messages that y'all have gotten? That has to account for something."

"Maybe, but it won't save another girl. I've got to get hard evidence."

Piper and Tessa stop the conversation because they know my mind is made up. Piper cranks up the radio and sings to the first song she likes. Tessa follows next in line, and I'm a beat behind her.

We spend the remainder of the day shopping, eating at P.F. Chang's, and heading back to Grassy Pond.

We arrive back home after dusk. Agreeing that we are better to tackle my parents as a team of three, we enter the house and try to make a break for it when Piper smells Mama's famous apple dumplings. She makes a wrong turn directly for the target we are trying to avoid.

"Pipe, what are you doin'?" I grit through my teeth.

"I'm eatin'. Those are the bomb diggity. I'll help you survive because it is totally going to be worth it once that first bite is in your mouth, and you know it!"

She is right. That buttery, flaky goodness is unbelievable. The three of us walk into the kitchen as Mama pulls the dumplings from the oven.

"Girls, y'all are right on time. Grab a plate and eat up! Your dad and I are going to watch a movie. Y'all wanna join?"

"Whatchawatchin'?" I ask.

"Some Clint Eastwood movie that's not been out too long. I can't think of the name, but it's supposed to be pretty good."

I look at both Piper and Tessa for an escape, and Piper decides to talk to my mama like only she can.

"Mama Number Two, you know we love a good chick flick, and I don't think that's one of them. We might just watch one in Charley's room."

Mama shakes her head as she scoops vanilla ice cream onto the dumplings. "It's so good to have y'all back in this house. It's just weird without all of you, ya know? Tessa, what's Sally been up to? I haven't seen her much since Char got home?"

"Oh, she's around, but she just wanted to give Char and me a little sister time. We're supposed to double date this weekend."

Grabbing our evening dessert, we make our way upstairs to my room and get comfortable on the bed. We turn on the TV and scan Netflix for an oldie but goodie. As I'm in the middle of a bite, my new prepaid phone signals that I have a text message.

Cash: Y'all back?

Me: Yeah, funny ur name is n contacts. lol

Cash: ☺we still meeting 2night? I'm dying 2 have u n my arms.

Me: u bet. we r watchin a movie right now. what time?

Cash: U want me 2 watch it 2?

Me: Sure let's not get caught.

"Dang girl, you got it bad. You better hope you don't look at that phone around Dylan if Cash texts you because it will be written all over your face."

I just shrug my shoulders and let them know that he's on his way. Of course, Piper is wondering if she and Tessa need to leave, but that's not the case.

A few minutes later, there's a light tapping on my window. I try to casually walk over to open it, but that doesn't happen. As I slide up the window, Cash kisses my lips and hops in.

"Ladies, how was Northlake?"

"Great, would have been better if we hit the lottery before we went," Piper announces.

"Yeah, I'm sure y'all would have loved that. So, what y'all watchin'?"

"*Hope Floats*," I say as we make our way back toward the bed. There's no way we can all fit on there, so Cash leans against the footboard and I ease myself between his legs. He wraps his arms around me, and I'm safe again.

After the movie, Piper excuses herself and goes home. Tessa exits to her own bedroom, and Cash and I stay still. I want to relish this moment with him, but I soon realize that I better lock the door. Knowing my luck, Mama will have to check-in before bed.

I move away from Cash, even though I'd rather not. I lock the door and walk back to Cash who has now stood up from the hard wooden floor.

"I think my ass fell asleep, but it was totally worth it."

I smile and make my way back to those strong, hardworking arms. We stand there in silence and just hold each other.

"Char-coal, I'm glad today was okay. I hope tomorrow is the same." He kisses my forehead and then places his forehead against mine. In this moment, I wish time would stand still, but that's not the case. Tomorrow is a new day, a day closer to Dylan's arrival, and one day closer to my freedom.

I look into Cash's eyes, place my hands on his cheeks, and pull his lips to mine. We lose ourselves for several minutes before he distances himself again.

"Char-coal, I better go. Sleep tight and text me after practice tomorrow. I love you."

"I will. I love you, too. Thank you for everything."

"What have I done, Char-coal? Except be your biggest fan. That's all I've ever been, but that's what you do when you love someone. You cheer for them through their highs and lows. Now, get some rest, and I'll meet you in your dreams."

"Can't you stay, Cash Money?"

Cash's eyes become the size of softballs. "Char, your parents would kill us. Plus, that's not gonna help your plan. Believe me. I'd love to hold you all night long, and I will one day. I'll hold you all night, and it will be the first night of forever."

Cash kisses me again, and backs away toward the window with our hands still interlaced. He lifts the window and crawls halfway out before stopping and kissing me again. Then, he makes his way out of the window, off the roof, and to his farm. I close the window and watch him as far as I can see.

I turn off my light, unlock the door, crawl into bed, and drift off into a deep slumber. My dreams are happy for the first time in a long time, and then I wake up to that sound I love to hate. Time for practice.

Chapter 13

Today the parking lot is fuller than yesterday. There must be more folks home, or the team's schedule has been changed. I shrug it off and make my way into the GPAC. This morning Molly is already in the pool area, Coach Stephens is on deck, and the lap swimmers are trucking down the lengths of the pool. I head into the locker room, change into my suit, go through my normal pre-swim rituals, and jump into the pool, following day two's workout.

Just like yesterday, the warm-up isn't bad at all, and then there are five sets to complete. They are like a perfect bar graph because set three just about kicked my rear and then it was downhill from there.

The final set, the backstroke, is my specialty, so I know it is going to be a breeze. It is two 100-meter backstrokes under 1:15 with a twenty-second break in between. *I got this!* Watching the clock, I prepare for the first 100-meters. Knowing it's my favorite and the event in which I shine the most, I decide to test myself just to see how fast I can really go. I push off the wall, kick as far as I can before turning up the heat, and move my arms in perfect motion. Once I reach the flags, I count to five and do a flip turn. Then pushing off, I thrust hard for the final leg. Counting from the flags, I push with all my might and once my fingertips touch the wall, I check the clock. It reads 1:12:34, but I know I can do better than that. I take my twenty-second break and go at it hard one more time. I am completely focused on beating the 1:10 marker, and it's going to happen.

Looking at the clock with five seconds to go, I take a deep breath, focus, and use every ounce of strength, desire, and emotion of the past few days and put it all into the water.

As I reach the flags, I can feel my calf muscles begin to burn, and I know I'm making great time. I flip and push with everything I have. On my final lap, I move my arms as fast as airplane propellers and kick my legs as hard as I can when I see the flags. I reach for the wall again, and just as I turn to look at the clock, I see him. Dylan Sloan is standing over my lane. Oh shit!

Standing there with his arms crossed and a smirk on his face, he starts talking before I can actually process that this is not a nightmare.

"Damn, Charley, that was a great time. 1:09:46. I guess you have been in the pool. You know, that text really got me thinking, and I had to get home as soon as possible," he says with a wink.

I take a deep breath and try to respond, knowing that this plan is going into effect one day early. This wasn't supposed to happen. I put on my big girl panties and realize this is what I have been waiting for. It's time to make a deal with the devil himself, and he's going down in the end.

"Thanks, I've been working my ass off if you want to know the truth. I'm hoping to make Olympic Trials this year," I say nonchalantly. "Well, I need to finish my workout." I reposition my goggles and get ready to start my cool-down. He is standing there at a loss for words. I didn't give him the time of day or gawk at his perfect body. I acted cool and shook him off like he was the Dylan before we started dating. I've definitely got him where I want him already.

After finishing the 200 choice cool-down, I remove my goggles and cap and place them onto the deck of the pool and dip my head back into the water like I do every day, but today is different. I know Dylan is watching, and I know what he likes so I turn it up just a notch. I don't look at him except from my peripheral vision, and it's evident that he notices.

Trying to hide the fact that I know I've got him looking, I hop out of the pool in one fluid motion and make my way to the locker room, shaking what my mama gave me on my way to get ready for the day. It's time to let Cash, Piper, and Tessa know that this plan is starting now.

Entering the locker room, the first thing I do is send a group text to Piper, Cash, and Tessa from the prepaid phone.

Me: Dylan's here. I'm k. B home n 30.

I put down the phone and begin to grab my shower stuff from my bag when the phone starts to blow up. The first text is from Cash, followed by Tessa, and then Piper. I assure them that I am fine, and we will talk as soon as I get home. I can't risk anyone overhearing anything.

I shower, get dressed and pack my bag to leave. As I open the door to the locker room, I almost jump out of my skin when Dylan startles me.

"Can you not scare people like that?"

"You know, Charley, it wasn't too long ago that you liked when I startled you in this hallway."

"Well, that was then, and this is now. Why aren't you in the pool anyways?"

"I just wanted to talk to you in private before you left. Make sure everything was okay."

Okay my ass. He is totally up to something.

"I'm good, but I gotta go. Piper's waiting on me. We got a little girl time planned this afternoon."

A flash of confusion runs across his face. "You mean you, Cash and Piper, right?"

"Um, no. I said girl time, Dylan. My life doesn't revolve around Cash."

A smile beams across his entire face, and I know I've got him hook, line, and sinker.

"So, I take it there is trouble in paradise?"

"There is no trouble because we aren't together. We haven't been for a while, if you recall. I like being away at school, and he wants me to stay in this little hicktown. I'm enjoying living life. Kinda like what you wanted me to do, but I was too much of a prude back then."

"Well, well, I find that a little odd, considering your strong values, but college changes folks. I've changed, just so you know."*I bet he has.*

"Oh, really? You wanna prove it?"

"I thought you'd never ask. So, what do you say if I pick you up tonight, and we catch up on what's been going on?"

"Aight, want to see if Tessa and Dustin want to hang with us?"

He must sense that I'm nervous because he gives in to that, or maybe because he's trying to play the good ol' boy card.

"I guess. Dustin and I will pick y'all up at seven."

"Sounds good." As I turn to leave, Dylan's hand brushes my arm. I get chill bumps, but not in a good way.

We go our separate ways, and I hurry to the car. I have got to get out of here before I lose it. I throw my bag into the car and break every speed limit on the way home.

Once I'm back at the farm, I notice that Mama's car is gone, and I'm thankful. I need to talk to Tessa without a chance of her eavesdropping. I hurry into the house and start to holler for Tessa. She is halfway down the steps before I even get the "T" out of my mouth.

"Char, are you okay? What did he say? Did he touch you? Are you sure you can do this, because I really don't think I can. I mean, I will if you still want to, but I don't know."

"TESS!" She stops mid-sentence of her rant. "I'm good; it's a day early, but I'm okay."

"Really? 'Cause I'd have wanted to chew him up and spit him out! Cash has already called and said you need to call him when you got here. Piper's on her way over."

"I'll call him in a minute, but we need to talk, just you and me." She gives me her best 'what the hell' look. That's when I explain our double date.

"Tessa, you have got to act like you like him, and that Cash is nothing to me. Do you understand that? You wear your feelings on your sleeves, and right now, we can't let that happen."

"I gotcha, Sis. I guess I'm jumping on the Team Dylan bandwagon for you only. I'll call Dustin and fill him in before Dylan gets home from the pool."

Tessa hurries back upstairs to call Dustin, and I call Cash.

"Hey, Cash Money."

"Char-coal, I'm so sorry you have to deal with this already. I just wanted one more day."

"Listen. If it wasn't today, it would be tomorrow, and then we would want another day. The sooner this starts, the faster it's over. But, you'll be proud to know that he's already falling right into my hands. This might be easier than I thought."

"Char, don't get too confident because you never know what that sick fucker is thinkin'."

"I know, but he totally believed that I was pissed at you. Oh, and we have a date tonight with Tessa and Dustin."

Cash doesn't say anything.

"Cash?"

"Char, something is so off about that. He's totally jumping right back on the Charley boat, and that's not his style. Be careful. I have a feeling that he has something up his sleeve."

"I will, and Dustin and Tessa will be there. I'm not putting myself alone with him unless it's absolutely necessary."

"It's not. Remember that. Do you know where you're going tonight?"

"No, but somehow I'll let you know." As Cash and I finish our conversation, I see Piper hauling ass down the gravel. "Um, Piper's here, so I guess I better get off the phone and explain it all to her. I'll let you know where we are and call you tonight when I get home. Okay? And, Cash Money, I love you. *Only* you."

"Be careful, Char-coal. I love you so much. I'll be waiting, and if you need me, I'll be there in a flash."

"Charley! Where are you?" Piper yells as the screen door slams behind her.

"I'm in the kitchen talkin' to Cash." Turning my attention back to Cash, we say our goodbyes once more and hang up.

Piper stands there impatiently tapping her foot for answers.

"Charley, what the hell? I thought we had one more day? One minute we're talking about a plan and the next it's in motion. I just can't handle this!" I look at her with complete surprise. Piper is never this tore up. She is an emotional wreck.

"Pipe, what's really goin' on?"

"It's Joe. He just called me and said that Dylan's making plans for you again. He sent him another creepy

118

message. This is too dangerous. You need to go to the cops now."

"What did he say? And when did he send it to him because he was getting ready to start his workout when I left."

"I'm guessing that as soon as your Honda was outta sight, he went back to being the same old Dylan. He called Joe this time and thanked him for all his hard work because you were falling right where he wanted you. Charley, that's freaky! Joe called me as soon as he hung up with him. He doesn't want anything to happen to you."

"Are you sure, or do you think this is part of Dylan's plan, too?"

Piper paces back and forth and turns on her heels so many times I lose count.

"Char, he's on our team. I'm positive. He has a good heart. Yes, he made a horrible mistake, but haven't we all? Please forgive him, and let's move on."

"I'm tryin', but I just want to be mad at him. Isn't that okay?"

"I know you do, but it's not right! If it were you, you wouldn't quit until he forgave you."

I don't say anything to that because I know she is exactly right. I turn and grab a Choice Cherry Gold from the fridge and toss her one as well. She pulls two packs of Fun Dip from her purse, and we sit at the table and eat in silence, but yet the silence fixes what is broken between us.

"Pipe, I'm sorry. You're right, but I just don't want to. I know he's got a good heart, but there are things that I thought I knew that I don't and that scares me. What if Dylan talks him into doing something else?"

"He's not. He doesn't want to lose you again or me for that matter. I believe in him, Char, and you should, too. Now, back to what's going on here. What are you going to do?"

Tessa be-bops in at the perfect time. "I'll tell ya what we're gonna do. It's called a double date."

Piper turns to look at me, and I nod my head yes.

"Well, I'd love to see how this goes. I think that's safe, Char, and don't be alone with him, not until you know it has to happen."

"I won't, Piper. I do need a favor tonight. I need you to text me while we're out and ask what I'm doing. Then, you can relay it to Cash. Sound good?"

"You got it!" I give her a hug, and we curl up on the couch and watch a few *ABC Family* Christmas movies before she leaves.

Piper gives Tessa and me hugs and then makes her way down the drive. Tessa and I look at each other. It's time to get all dressed up because we have somewhere to be tonight. Plan Take Dylan Sloan Down is about to be in full swing.

Chapter 14

Right on time, Dylan and Dustin pull into the driveway. Knowing that I'm about to get back into the car that started my night from hell gives me goose bumps. Tessa must sense it, too. She looks at me with questioning eyes, and I just smile.

Mama and Dad are in the kitchen. We've tried to keep them in the dark as much as possible. The less time I have here with them and less questioning, the better.

"Mama! Dad! We'll be back by eleven!" Tessa yells.

"Hold up, young ladies. Where are you going?" Dad asks as he makes his way toward us in the foyer.

"We have a double date tonight with Dustin and Dylan." Dad looks at me like his head is about to spin.

"You're what?"

"Goin' on a double date," I say.

"Charley, are you okay? I know that was bad with Cash, but to just jump ship back to Dylan? I don't think it's a good idea."

"Dad, I'm fine. He's home for break and wants to go out. No big deal. Plus, this way I can keep an eye on Tessa for ya!"

Dad looks at me with questioning eyes, but shakes his head and walks back to the kitchen.

"Girls, be home no later than eleven and call me if you need me. Got it?"

As soon as those words are said, there is a knock at the door. *OMG! Really? He's actually going to talk to my parents.* I begin to walk toward the door when I see my mama making a beeline for the foyer. *Shit.*

Tessa and I walk to the front door, and I push open the screen.

Dylan and Dustin are standing there with bouquets of flowers, dressed like they are taking us somewhere totally not in Grassy Pond.

"Hello, Mrs. Rice, how are you?" Dylan asks with sweet Southern charm.

"I'm good, Dylan. How about yourself? School going okay?"

"Yes, ma'am, I'm good and school's great. Thanks for letting Charley go out with me tonight."

"You're very welcome. Dustin, it's good to see you. Make sure they are home by eleven."

They say, "Yes, ma'am," in unison. Mama gives me a look that only I understand. It's a look of question, concern, and one that says, call me if you need me.

"Mama, can you put these in a vase for us?"

"Sure." She turns and walks into the kitchen, and we make our way out of the house.

Once the door shuts behind us, the four of us let out a deep breath. Are we all that uncomfortable? Dylan takes his hand and gestures for me to go first. Where is Dylan?

This nice guy is definitely not him. I nod and make my way down the steps, followed by Tessa and the guys.

Once we are in the yard, we pair up. Dustin takes Tessa by the hand, and I'm beginning to panic just thinking about Dylan's hand on mine.

As we reach the Mustang, Dylan makes his way to the passenger seat and opens the door in one suave motion. He has this game down to an art. When I approach him, he takes me by the hand and kisses it. *Yuck! I need some hand sanitizer!* It is amazing how much effort it takes to keep my feelings in check when all I really want to do is go ape shit on this total asshole, and that is putting it nicely.

"What was that for, Dylan?"

"Can't a guy try to make up for being such a jerk?"

I look at him as if he has lost his damn mind, but then turn on a little Southern charm of my own.

"Then you better start doing a lot of ass kissin', Prince Charming," I say in the sweetest, thickest Southern accent as possible.

"There's the Charley I've been lookin' for." As he bows, I slide into my seat. Then he winks, closes the door, and walks with confidence around to the driver's side.

Once inside the car, Dylan asks what we should do tonight. *Strange.*

"In all the years I've known you, Dylan Sloan, I've never known you to ask what someone wants to do. What has gotten into you?"

"Let's just say that I've realized that it's not always about me. I've been workin' on that. Right, Dustin?"

"Yeah, he has, Charley. You'd be surprised. He even let me have the last piece of MeeMaw's pound cake today. I about fell out!"

I turn my head to Dustin. "Really? You gave him the last piece of pound cake? Something is definitely wrong with you."

"No, I'm just trying to be more open to people and not be so in control of everything."

Well, that light mood just went dark for me with that one word. *Control.* He has to have control, be in charge, always on top, first at everything, and now I know this is a total game for him, too. I've got to turn up my Southern charm and acting skills.

"I think that's a smart move, Dylan, because we can't control life. It's kinda outta our hands, ya know?"

"Yeah, I know. So, Bro, where are we goin'?"

"I was thinkin' maybe we need to get out of Grassy Pond for a bit. Y'all wanna go check out some Christmas lights and eat dinner in the city?"

"City? Like big city, Charlotte?" Tessa questions playfully.

"Yeah, the Speedway's got the mega light show. I thought it would be fun since it's not but a few blocks away. Then again, traffic could be a mess. I was thinkin' maybe Wild Wings for supper?"

I'm thinking that at least it isn't Hooter's, because after what happened in that parking lot with Cash, I'd never be able to keep my game face on.

"Um, chicken feathers covered in Garlic! Garlic! Garlic! I'm in," I say.

"Well, I know where my lips won't be." Dylan laughs, and I cringe.

"You know it's to keep the vampires away because I'm totally a werewolf fan."

"Damn right, Char. Team Jacob all the way!" Tessa exclaims. We both laugh, and Dustin pipes back in.

"Well, maybe we should change these plans if it's gonna be all about Shark Boy tonight," Dustin comments.

As much as I hate to admit it, it used to be fun with Dylan before he wanted to have sex and before that night. He had been my kick ass and take names partner on the team. We were always first in our events, had confidence in what we did, and we just made sense, even if everyone else couldn't believe I actually got him. Needless to say, if he keeps up the pre-Charley and Dylan act, he is definitely making this easier on me.

"So, Wild Wings and the Speedway?" We all agree and make our way on 85N to Charlotte.

The conversation is light, and the music is loud. I'm comfortable in this car, knowing my act won't be too difficult tonight and my sister is by my side.

As we cross over the lake, my iPhone chirps inside my purse, and I know it's either Piper or Mama. I'm right, but I wasn't expecting Mama.

Mama: Charley, I've got a weird feeling. Please be careful. Call me if you need me no matter what it is. I love you both!

Me: we r good. Going to wild wings and 2 c lights @ speedway. Luv u.

Mama: love u 2.

"Tessa, that was Mama makin' sure of our plans. You know she is so dang nosey."

"What are we gonna do with her, Charley? We are going to be sixty years old, and she's still gonna wanna know our every move."

I just shake my head. After placing my phone back into my purse, I put it in the floorboard. I relax in the seat when I hear Bruno Mars "Gorilla" come on the radio. Immediately, my senses are heightened and I'm taken back to the actuality of my life. This song blared through the speakers while Dylan and I left the party at Trent's. It was the night my life changed forever. I try my best not to react, but I can see Dylan respond as well. It looks as if every vein is struggling to stay within his rock hard body. It's almost as if he wants to change the station, but that would be weird because Tessa is rockin' out in the backseat. We are the only two that have a clue as to the meaning of this party song. He doesn't say anything. Instead, he takes one hand and finds mine. He wraps his palm over the top of mine, and as it starts to sweat, he intertwines our fingers and gives them a firm squeeze. At this point, I don't know if it's an "I'm sorry" squeeze or an

"I'll be back for more" squeeze. Either way, it has gotten my nerves all out of whack, and I can't wait for Tessa to shut up, the song to end, and Dylan to get his slime ball hands off me.

The song comes to an end, and Dylan rubs his thumb against mine. *What the hell?* I look at him and grin because honestly I have no clue what to do. I can't yank it away, but I don't want him to think I'm going to give him another piece of this, ever!

When the last beat stops, it's as if a two-ton elephant has left the car. I can't even believe how grateful I am to hear "Bubble Butt" next on the radio playlist because I hate that damn song. Really? I mean, who comes up with shit like that?

I notice that we are making our way toward the Panthers stadium and Center City. WTH? Wouldn't the Wild Wings at the university be better for the lights?

"Why aren't we going to the Wild Wings at the university? That one's closer to the Speedway,"

I ask, trying to keep my cool.

"Oh, Dylan thought it might be nice to walk around the Epic Center tonight," Dustin says because he is clueless as to what is at the Epic Center. "I wanted to check it out and see if we can get a glimpse at Junior."

"Oh." Is all I can manage because the Junior he is referring to is Dale, Jr., and where would we see him? Whiskey River.

Tessa chimes in right on time, "Now, Dustin, do you really think that he's gonna be there? We are going to Wild

Wings, not that club of his. And, anyways, it's too early for shit like that. People like him aren't makin' an appearance right now. I mean, nice thought and all, but it ain't happening."

I love my sister. I love my sister. I could continue to repeat that in my head all day. I know we are going to Center City because we are already there, but I'm avoiding Whiskey River at all costs.

As we drive down Tryon Street, I can't help but think about all the trips in the Love Machine. I start to smile and Dylan notices.

"So, the big city is good for you, huh?"

"It's more like the memories. We come here a lot to dance and stuff."

"Oh, too bad we haven't run into each other. You know we haven't really talked much, and I didn't go where I planned either. In fact, I'm going to Davidson now. I just needed smaller, but their team is kick ass."

I think all the blood has left my body. No wonder I always felt like he was close. He was. No more than a damn thirty-minute drive.

"That's good."

"Yeah, I didn't know you were on the team, but I guess it might make it interesting for Southern States this year?"

"Yeah, I guess."

"Guess we won't be on the same team, but just so you know, I'll still pull for ya."

"Oh, I bet because you never pull for anyone on the other team. That's like a Carolina fan pullin' for Duke. It's not gonna happen."

Tessa's eyes are about to bug outta her head when I glance over my shoulder. Dustin comes to our rescue before Dylan sees the terror in her eyes. Dustin pulls her in and starts to make out with her.

"Bro, do y'all need a hotel room or something?" Dustin doesn't comment; he just lets Tessa get lost in his lips.

Within minutes, we are parking in the deck and walking into Wild Wings. There isn't much of a wait, so we have a seat. More small talk is exchanged, and when the waitress calls for our table, Dylan places his hand onto my lower back as we make our way.

We order and eat. The guys enjoy the basketball game on the TVs, and we actually have a good time. Then, my phone chirps again. Piper.

Piper: what u up 2?

Me: Charlotte @WW then going to c lights @ CMS.

Piper: Nice! Call me later!

"Who was that?" Dylan questions.

"Piper, of course. She's going through Charley withdrawals. Since we're at different schools, when we're home, we try to make up for it. I think she and Justin are goin' to Turtle's tonight."

"Maybe we can stop by there when we get back."

"I'm game. What about y'all?" I ask as I look to Tessa and Dustin.

They look at each other and shrug their shoulders. "Sure," they say in unison.

"Y'all are like the cutest couple, ever. Just so you know," I say. "How long until we head to the Speedway?"

"I'd say we probably should head that way in about fifteen," Dustin says as he looks at Dylan for guidance.

He answers between bites of his wing, "Sounds good to me."

Dinner was pleasantly nice and doable. Before we leave, Tessa and I excuse ourselves to the ladies' room. We have a full-out conversation mid-stream about the ride, supper, and what happens if we go to Turtle's. My biggest question is, will Cash be there? On most Saturday nights, if he's not at the club or with me, he's at Turtle's.

Dylan and Dustin are waiting by the door when we leave the restroom. Dustin opens the door and holds it as we exit. I glance to my right, and there it is, Whiskey River. The saddest part about this whole scenario is not only have I never been inside, but now Dylan has this first memory for me as well. Damn him!

"Hey, can we at least check out the merchandise?" Dustin asks.

Tessa, Dylan, and I look at each other like, *really?* But, we let him. He's a total Dale, Jr. fan. Dustin pulls open the door, and we make our way to the merchandise table. The place is a typical club scene where the girls working are wearing black leather vests with nothing underneath, short shorts, boots, and cowboy hats. No wonder the guys like this place. The music isn't country all the way, but a good variety. I notice a mechanical bull in the corner and can't help but think who would have been on that if we would have made it here. I can only assume all of us would have at some point. Dylan pulls me from my thoughts.

"Charley, are you okay? You seem a little spacey."

"Yeah, I've just wanted to come here, but we haven't yet."

"Oh, we have only been here once and that was the night before Study Day," Dylan replies.

My world stops. I now know why Joe told me. He was protecting me from the truth. He knew that Dylan would be here, and shit was going to go down. A wave of emotion crashes into me, and I have to regain my composure before it shows. Tessa glances my way, and her face is a flash of fear.

"Well, I guess that would have been an interesting night, huh?"

"Yeah, it would have, 'cause Charley, you would have been mine that night," Dylan whispers into my ear and chills run down my spine.

"I thought I've always been yours, Dylan?" I form the words as a question.

He smiles. "Now, that's the Charley I've been waiting on."

Chapter 15

"Aight, I've bought all I'm gonna buy. Let's go see some lights!" Dustin says. He's completely oblivious to what just happened, but Tessa isn't.

"Yeah, let's get outta here. I wanna see the lights!" Tessa says sweetly as she snuggles up to Dustin.

"Me, too." I wrap my arm into Dylan's, and we make our way to the Mustang. Now that my emotions are in check, and I know that I can trust Joe, this game has just been taken up a level. I can't wait to tell Piper, and it's time to turn up the charm with Dylan.

Dylan looks my way and smiles. He opens the passenger door and makes his way around to the driver's side. He slides in, buckles up, cranks the ignition, and we are on our way to the Speedway. Thank goodness. As we travel to the other side of Charlotte, I enjoy the lights of the city. I glance at Dylan, and he gives me that perfect grin. I smile back and decide to continue to play this game. I slide my hand to reach Dylan's and intertwine our fingers. The confidence that he has always possessed is definitely glowing. He takes his thumb and glides it up and down mine. I can't even believe that I'm allowing him to touch me, let alone, act like I'm enjoying it. I can't wait for the day he pays.

The line to get into the Speedway is backed to infinity. I look at Tessa, Dustin, and Dylan to see if they are thinking what I'm thinking.

"No, Char, we aren't leavin'," Tessa says.

"Really? I mean, we can go check out the trailer park near the house for free, and there's no traffic."

"No, we're here, and we're gonna enjoy it, even if it takes all night," Dylan says with a grin. I can't help but feel an underlying current with that comment.

As we make our way inside, it is overwhelming the number of lights that are in this place. There are millions upon millions of lights on display, *The Polar Express* is playing on the biggest TV screen known to man, and there are all kinds of activities going on in the infield. There is a nativity scene, petting zoo, and a chance to have your picture made with Santa.

"Y'all, this is totally worth the wait. It's ah-maz-ing! Plus, we are actually driving on the track of the Coca-Cola 600," I say.

"Too bad we can't put the pedal to the metal. I'd love to see how fast she'd go," Dylan says as he glides his hand over the dashboard.

"There's a thing called the Richard Petty Driving Experience. That's how you can do that, ya know?" Tessa smarts back.

I look out the window, cover my mouth with my hand and try to hide my giggle, but it's totally not working.

"What? Is something funny, Charley?" Dylan questions.

I shake my head no, and Tessa adds her two cents.

"Oh, it's funny all right. It's a cryin' shame a car with this much power has to go ten miles an hour when most drivers are hitting well above a hundred."

"Tess, take it easy on my brother. It's not his fault that he's helping me live out my dream, but at a snail's pace." He begins to laugh as well.

"Well, I'm glad ya'll find this funny. I didn't realize this was going to be a pick on Dylan kinda night, but whatever." There is an ounce of what sounds like hurt in Dylan's voice, but most of it is irritation.

"Hey, Dylan, you know we're just kiddin'," I say as I slide a little closer to him. That seems to take his mind off his previous thought.

After making a lap around the track, we park and enjoy the nativity scene, live petting zoo, and Tessa and I even have our picture made with Santa.

It's getting cold out, and I'm about worn out from this game I'm playing. We make our way back to the Mustang and return to Grassy Pond.

"So, are we still planning on hitting up Turtle's?" Tessa asks.

As I yawn a yes, everyone looks at me for reassurance

"Charley, that doesn't sound like you're up to it. You sure you don't want to call it a night?" Tessa asks.

"Nah, I'm good. Just been a long day with practice and all. I'll be aight."

Throughout the remainder of the way to Turtle's Pool Hall, Dylan continues to keep his eyes on me. It's almost as if he wants to get into my head and know exactly what I'm thinking. Well, I'm thinking one thing and one thing only. I sure hope Cash isn't here, because for him to hear me talk about what is going on is one thing, but to see it firsthand isn't fair.

Once we hit the county line, we make our way to the crossroads and pull into the parking lot at Turtle's. Nothing has changed since my last visit. However, I hope tonight doesn't end like the last time.

Dylan opens the door, and I see Sammy working the bar. He throws up a hand to welcome us, but there is a slight hesitation when he sees who's with me.

We make our way to the bar.

"Glad you're back, Charley," Sammy says as he hands me a Choice Cherry Gold.

"Now, how'd you know that's what I'd want? I might have changed it up," I say with a little flirtation in my voice.

"Hun, you've been drinkin' the same beverage since you stepped foot in here. Honestly, I can't wait until you turn twenty-one because I wanna know what you're gonna add to it."

I blush at that idea because I already know. As soon as Dylan sees my reaction, he moves in closer, puts his arm around me and stakes his claim. He even seals the deal by kissing my cheek. His lips are like ice on my warm skin, and I can't wait for them to break away from my body. Instead, I lean closer in and make him believe that I am all about Dylan Sloan.

There are two open pool tables near the back of Turtle's. We grab our drinks, a pool stick, and a table.

"So, how are we teaming up tonight?" I ask.

"I think we should play guys against girls," Tessa says.

"I'm game with that. What about you, Bro?"

"Sounds good to me. Let's show these ladies not to mess with the Sloan brothers. Ladies, you go first."

Tessa racks the balls, and we prepare for a game that's sisters against brothers. Tessa breaks and, of course, has to get solids. We high five, and it's game on. Each time it's our turn, we make sure we lean a little farther across the table, show off the girls, and make the boys drool. They try their best to gain our attention, but they are no match for the Rice sisters.

We finish the first game and win with no problem. That's when I hear the sweetest voice in the distance. *Do not turn around. Do not react.* Cash Money is here and I have to act like I hate him. This isn't going to be fun.

"Y'all ready for round two?" I ask as I ignore Cash talking to Sammy.

"Sure," Dylan says as he walks up beside me, slides his hand into my back pocket, and pulls me in to show his ownership.

Round two isn't as nice for us, but I'm sure it has to do with the fact that Cash is watching. I've tried my best not to look his way, but that's damn near impossible.

"Aight, we're tied up. One more game and we are calling it quits. I'm exhausted," I tell Dylan.

The last game goes in our favor, but only because I know the night is coming to an end. Tessa and I continue to employ our assets to help us win. We use a little hip bump as our winning move.

Dustin walks up behind Tessa, takes the pool stick from her, places it onto the table, and pulls her in for one of the hottest kisses I've ever seen. My dad would die! I'm about to blush when I hear Cash yell at her. "How 'bout y'all get a room!" I laugh and look at Cash. Dylan looks at me with curiosity, but then he does something I hadn't expected today.

Dylan takes my pool stick, returns it to the wall where it belongs, walks back to me, and slides his hand to my cheek as he stares into my eyes. He eyes are full of hunger, and before I can think about how I will react, he places his lips onto mine. He starts slow and tender and then becomes more feverous. I want to break away, to tell him to stop, but if I do, this game is over. I can't afford that, but I also don't want to hurt the man of my dreams who has to watch it first- hand.

I begin to slow the kisses and pull away. When our lips part, I notice that Dylan looks over my shoulder and smiles. My heart breaks because he did that to show Cash he had me, and now everyone in Grassy Pond will know that Dylan and I are a couple... again.

I turn around and see Cash throw his drink into the trash, but not before he looks my way. Never in my life have I seen that much hurt on his face, and as much as I want to run after him, I can't. Instead, I move myself closer to Dylan, wrap my arms around his waist and snuggle into his chest. The tension in the air is thick, but exactly what is expected.

Tessa and Dustin finally come up for air and realize what has gone down. "Hey, I think it's time to call it a night. Y'all ready?" Dustin asks. As we make our way out of Turtle's, every eye is on us, and I know that everyone is asking themselves the same question. Dylan opens the door for me again and then makes his way around to the driver's side. While he is walking around, I feel my cellphone buzz, and I know without a doubt it's Cash. The ride back to the farm is quiet, and I play it off as being tired. Tessa follows suit by resting her head on Dustin's shoulder.

Once back at the farm, we get out of the car. Dustin and Tessa walk toward the house, and I start to follow when Dylan grabs my hand and holds me back.

"Char, hold up a minute." I turn and face him. "Thanks for tonight. I had a good time, and I'm sorry if things moved faster than you planned."

Placing my hands into my front pockets and raising one hip higher than the other, I gather my thoughts.

"You know me too well. I've always been about taking things slowly, but tonight, that was genius with Cash." I walk toward Dylan and wrap my arms around his neck, leaving him with a kiss and wanting more. When I know I've given him just enough, I pull away and walk myself to the house, passing Dustin on the way. I turn and wave as I walk inside.

Mama and Dad are asleep in their usual locations in the living room. I make a mad dash for the bathroom because everything I ate tonight is about to come up, and there isn't enough mouthwash in this house to kill the germs I have in my mouth!

After I sanitize myself the best I can, I look into the mirror and see myself for what I truly am. I am no better than Dylan. I'm a liar, and I've hurt the most important person in my life. It's time to face this reality and call Cash.

Removing my prepaid phone from my purse, I look at the text.

Cash $: Charley meet me at the club a.s.a.p.!

Tears stream down my face, my hands begin to shake, and I reply with one letter.

Me: K

Wiping my eyes, I open the door and Tessa is standing there ready to say something, but as soon as she sees my face, she says nothing. She just pulls me into a tight embrace and tells me that everything will be okay. I pull away from her and let her know that I have to meet Cash.

I change into more comfortable attire before I make my way to my four-wheeler. Once I'm out of range of my parents' ears, I punch the gas and hurry to the club.

I can see the light in the distance, and my heart begins to beat faster the closer I get. I jump off and hurry up the ladder. Cash is standing by the window, gazing at the pond. He turns and looks at me as I reach the doorway of the club.

"Cash, I'm…" Cash stops me mid-sentence by crashing his lips unto mine. The waterworks start and continue until he pulls away from me.

"Char-coal, I'm so sorry. If I'd have known he was going to do that in front of everyone, I would have stayed home."

"You're sorry? Cash, what I did was cold-hearted, unfair, and makes me no better than Dylan."

Taking his hand, Cash cups my face. "You are nothing like him, and I know the real you. But, that did hurt like hell, and I don't think it's gonna get any easier. He doesn't know you're here, does he?" I shake my head no. "Good. Because you are staying here until we have to go home. I love you, Char-coal, and no one will change that."

"I love you, too, and you have no idea how relieved I am to be with you right now. I honestly don't know if I can do this. I mean, play two different people. Tonight wore me out!"

"I have faith in you, and it will work out. Just know that no matter what, I know where your heart belongs and no one can take that away from me."

There aren't any more words exchanged; instead, Cash holds me in his arms. We cherish the night and each other until the sun beings to rise.

Chapter 16

Hurrying back home, I know that I'm cutting it close. Dad is liable to be out and about on the farm already, and if he spots me leaving from the club, this game is over before it's even started. I park the four-wheeler and hear the screen door open on the porch. *Shit!* I hide behind the shed, and once Dad is out of sight, I run to the house.

Once inside, I realize the remainder of the house is quiet. *Yes!* I tiptoe upstairs and crawl back into bed, but before I do, I text Cash.

Me: TY Cash $ I <3 u 4ever!

Cash: Char-coal u will always b my 4ever!

I roll over, close my eyes, and drift off to sleep until the smell of bacon hits my nostrils. Stopping by the bathroom, I check myself in the mirror. I don't look too bad, but Mama is likely to ask questions. I decide to request backup, and I make my way into Tessa's room.

"Tess, wake up. It's time for breakfast." She pulls her covers over her head, "Char, leave me alone."

"Tess, really. I need you. Mama's gonna ask twenty questions, and I need a backup." Taking a deep breath, she throws her comforter off and rolls out of bed. Pointing her finger at me, she tells me, "You owe me, and this list just keeps getting longer. Oh, and how did it go last night?"

"Actually, better than I expected. Tessa, I thought he was going to be furious, but instead, he melted away the poison Dylan put on my lips last night."

"Okay, stop right there. I don't need to hear anymore. So, are you ready to face the woman that knows all?"

"I guess."

We slowly make our way downstairs. Mama glances over her shoulder when we enter the kitchen, then she returns to the stove.

"Mornin', girls. Breakfast is almost ready. Y'all have fun last night? I noticed y'all didn't wake us when you got home. I woke up this morning with the biggest crick in my neck."

"Sorry, Mama, but y'all were out," I say.

Tessa chimes in, "Yeah, we tried, but y'all didn't budge."

About that time, my phone chirps.

Piper: Have fun last night? I heard it was explosive! I'm getting ready and then on my way.

Me: Kinda, Yup, Sounds good.

As I place my phone back onto the table, I realize that I have got to get in my workout. Now, I'm off schedule, and I better text Piper back.

Me: Totally slept in, gotta swim, meet me at 12.

Piper: Hurry it up! I need details!

I scarf down breakfast and jump up like I'm late for school.

"Charley, how was last night?" Mama asks as I'm putting my plate into the sink.

"Good actually. Wasn't it, Tess? We went to see the lights at the Speedway. They were amazing! Mama, I felt like I was in a snow globe."

"That's good, Char, but I feel like something's not right. I know that it's none of my business, and you don't have to tell me, but I feel like you're not telling me something. Just know you can talk to me." Mama picks up her coffee and continues like it's nothing, but I know better. She wants answers.

"Mama, things didn't go well with Dylan before, but I'm trying to give him a second chance. Cash really pissed me off. He can't tell me what I can and can't do. I'm just enjoying life and taking it one day at a time. And, yes, I know I can talk to you. I gotta go. I can't believe I slept in."

"Sweet girl, don't you know it's okay to rest sometimes? Now, go kick some butt in the water, and let me know your plans for the day."

"Okay." I hurry back upstairs, grab my swim bag, hurry down the stairs, and put the Honda in the wind.

As I pull into the GPAC, I spot Dylan's Mustang first. *Shit!* Pull it together, Charley. It's time to put that game face back on. I grab my bag, toss it over my shoulder, and enter the GPAC with my head held high and enough confidence to stop anyone that crosses my path.

Heading into the locker room, I see Dylan already in the water. He notices me and smiles before starting his next set. I change and make my way on deck.

I take an extra few minutes to stretch, making sure that Dylan notices before I begin my workout. Today, my workout is more therapeutic than anything. It's exactly what I need in order to deal with the stress that is in the water with me. After I finish my sets, I hear Dylan holler at me.

"You looked great out there, Char."

"Thanks."

We both make our way to the locker room, and I hurry and shower. I pull my hair up into a messy bun, knowing I can fix it once I get home. I toss my towel, suit, cap, and goggles into my bag and push open the door, only to be attacked by Dylan Sloan. My first instinct is to scream, but then I recall a previous memory.

I start to laugh as his lips faintly touch mine, but then he pauses.

"What?" I question. "Haven't we been here before?"

He smiles, and then tries to conquer my lips again. I let him get a feel for about two seconds, and then I totally replay that scene. I push away from him, leaving my hands on his chest.

"You know Coach will kill us. Plus, I gotta meet Piper. She's got big plans for us or something." I give him a brief peck on the lips and then hurry to my car.

Once I'm inside the car, I pull my towel from my bag and wipe my lips. I think I'm gonna have to carry mouthwash and sanitizer at all times. Those items are definitely on our to-do list today.

At home, I hurry upstairs to get ready for the day. I quickly dry my hair and then hurry outside to see if Dad needs any help before Piper and I head out for the day. He needs someone to check on the horses in the barn. I make my way to the barn, feed them, and make it back with time to spare before Piper arrives.

"Hey, Pipe. What are we up to today?"

"I was thinking a little Christmas shopping is in order. Plus, I need the scoop on last night. From what I heard, Cash was pissed when he left Turtle's."

"That would be an understatement, but I made up for it later."

Mama comes around the corner, and Pipers mouths, "O-M-G!"

"Mama, we're going shopping and then just hang out. We might go to the movies or something."

"Sounds good. Be careful and stay out of trouble."

Piper insists on driving, so I can spill my details from last night. I tell her everything from supper, the Speedway, and Turtle's to my late night with Cash.

"Char, how long do you think this is going to have to continue?"

"I'm not sure, but at least I know I can trust Joe." Piper whips her car off the road and parks it.

"What do you mean, Charley?"

"Oh, I left out that detail, didn't I?" I say with a smirk. "Dylan informed me that he would have been at Whiskey River that night. Joe was protecting me. That's why he confessed."

Piper takes her hands and beats on the steering wheel with excitement. "We have got to call him! I knew it!"

Piper takes out her phone, hits Joe in the contacts, and then passes the phone to me.

"Hey, Piper," Joe says sweetly.

"Um, hey, Jackalope Joe." I pause and wait for his reaction.

"Squirrel? Is that you?"

"Yup, I'm sorry that I didn't believe you."

"Oh my gosh, I can't believe you actually called. What changed your mind?"

"Well, I know why you told me that night. You were protecting me. I know Dylan was going to be at Whiskey River, and you didn't want whatever his plan was to take place."

"Squirrel, I just couldn't let anything happen to you. I didn't care what you thought of me. I just couldn't let you go there." He stops for a second and begins to speak again, "How did you find out?"

Taking a deep breath, I look at Piper, swallow hard, and then explain. "I'm kinda acting like I want to be with him again."

"What the hell do you mean by that?"

"I want him to pay, and I'm going to get proof of what a scumbag he really is, and then I'm taking him down. Piper, Tessa, and Cash are helping me."

"I don't like that at all! He's dangerous. Don't put yourself in a bad position."

"I'm not. Tessa and Dustin went on a double date with us last night. Oh, and I'm happy for you and Piper, even if I gave her hell to start."

"Thanks, but you are our priority. How long do we have to go along with this game?"

"If all goes as planned, it will be by Southern States, if not sooner."

"Squirrel, that's like two months away."

"I know. Well, here's Piper." I decide to cut him off because I don't want to discuss it anymore. Piper and Joe finish their conversation, and before we know it, we are at Northlake for some much needed retail therapy.

We spend the remainder of the afternoon in and out of stores. As we make our way to the car, we each have our hands full and are struggling. Piper drops her bag of shoes about fifteen feet from the car. I start laughing, and then I lose one as well. We look like a bunch of crazies. We grab our bags and finally make it to the car.

"Ohmygawsh, Piper. That wore my ass out! The only thing I need now is a bed, and I'd be out like a light!"

"I'm just glad all this Christmas shopping is finished."

"Me too. So, what are we doing tonight?"

"I'm thinking a pizza and movie at my house. Whatcha think, Piper?"

"I'm game."

We sing every song on the Christmas station, and I laugh so hard that I almost pee my pants during Piper's rendition of "Santa Baby". Before we know it, we are back in Grassy Pond and I'm no longer tired. We decide that a movie night is still in order. We stop at Piper's house to grab her clothes and her makeup because she can't do without it.

At the Chevron, we grab a Hunt Brother's pizza fully loaded with all the meat, cheese and triple bacon. The aroma is making my stomach growl as I steal a bite of topping. Piper slaps the box lid when she catches me.

Once we are at the farm, we stop in the kitchen to grab drinks, plates, napkins, and dessert. Then, we make our way to the living room, sprawl out on the couch and turn on *ABC Family* for whatever movie is on tonight and pig out.

By piece number three, I'm stuffed and that makes me sleepy. Mama, Tessa, and Dad hang out with us, and this reminds me of so many nights before I left for Southern. I sure do miss when things were simple.

Once the movie ends, we make our way upstairs. We watch another movie on Netflix, but this time it's just a good ol' chick flick. Halfway through the movie, my phone rings. It's Dylan.

"Hey."

"Hey, what are you and Piper up to tonight?"

"We're watching a chick flick. What about you?"

"Oh, Trent and I were just out riding around and thought we might stop by."

"You can if you want to, but you know we'll have to hang out downstairs."

He laughs, "The rents are still pissed at me, huh?"

"Yeah, they are, but it's okay. Let me see if Piper cares." I look at Piper whose eyes are huge, but knows we have to go along with it. "She doesn't care. We'll meet you downstairs."

"Okay, we'll see y'all in ten."

I hit *End* and Piper lays into me.

"I know, Piper. I know, but we have to make it look real."

"You know your parents are going to be pissed. It's getting late."

"As long as we stay downstairs or hang out on the porch, we'll be good." Piper is unsure, and sends Cash a text to let him know what's going on.

We both take a minute to freshen up before going to meet them downstairs. I stop by Tessa's room to let her know what's going on, and she's game. Once we see the headlights coming down the gravel, we make our way to the front door only to be stopped by my mama.

"Girls, where are you going?"

"Dylan and Trent are just stopping by for a few minutes. We are just going to hang out on the porch or in the living room, if that's okay?"

"Your dad and I are going to bed, but I'd feel better if you were inside. Make sure they are gone by midnight."

"Thanks, Mama." I give her a hug goodnight, but she pauses and waits for a greeting with Dylan.

Dylan knocks on the door, and I open it. Dylan and Trent are standing there in jeans, boots, thermal long sleeves, and toboggans. If this were two years ago, I would have had to pick my mouth off the floor. I smile and tell them to come in.

"Hey, Mrs. Rice. Thanks for letting us stop by. I didn't get to talk to Charley much today at the pool."

"You're welcome, Dylan. Just make sure you are gone by midnight."

"Yes, ma'am," they say in unison.

Mama goes into the kitchen to fix her coffee for in the morning, and then she excuses herself upstairs to go to bed. Dad is already asleep by now.

I ask the guys if they want something to drink or any of the leftover pizza, and of course, they do. We walk into the living room and watch another movie on Netflix. This time it's not a chick flick, but rather an action one.

I snuggle into Dylan's arm on the loveseat while Piper and Trent sit at opposite sides of the couch. I catch myself dozing off, but am awakened when I hear the clock strike midnight.

"I guess that's our cue," Trent says.

Piper and I walk them to the door, and Trent makes his way outside, allowing Dylan to stay behind. Piper walks into the kitchen, and I could kill her about now, but it's part of the act.

"Thanks for stopping by tonight," I say as Dylan pulls me in for a tight hug and then brushes his lips on mine. Piper helps keep it short by interrupting. *That's my girl!* Then, he distances himself from me and our hands are the last thing to separate. He turns as he walks down the steps, and I close the door. Once he is in the car, I lock the door, turn off the porch light, and make a mad dash for the bathroom again. Sanitize, mouthwash, and repeat.

Both Tessa and Piper are waiting in my bedroom when I'm finished. They have sadness in their eyes. I sit on the bed with them and cry a good, hard, much needed cry.

As if right on cue, there is a tapping on my window, and my knight is standing there with a Choice Cherry Gold and a PB&J. I wipe away the tears as Tessa opens the window.

"Hey, Tessa, you wanna show me that new book you just downloaded?" Piper says.

"Sure, we'll be in my room."

The door clicks closed, and I fall into Cash Money's arms.

"Hold up a minute, or you're gonna be wearing this PB&J. I thought it might help you feel better. I know it's not Fun Dip, but that's yours and Piper's thing."

I smile a half-smile as I glance up to the best man I've ever known, both inside and out. I pull him tighter because I'm not sure how he knew, but he knew I needed him. Then, fear enters my body.

"You don't think he knows you're here, do you?"

"No, he doesn't. I made sure that I saw those taillights hit the paved road and were out of sight. I even parked the four-wheeler at the club and walked up here."

"Really? You could have parked it behind the barn."

"Char-coal, I can't risk anything when it comes to you. I've been watching from a distance. I know what I'm getting you for Christmas." I look at him quizzically. "A gallon or two of mouthwash. Every time his lips touch these, I want to beat him to a pulp. As much as I hate to say this, I wish this would hurry up. Do you really think it's going to take until Southern States?"

"I don't know, but I really hope it doesn't. I'm struggling, and it's been a week!"

Cash pulls me closer and runs his strong, hardworking hands through my hair. I can feel his heart pounding. This isn't just about me; it's about us.

He takes my chin, lifts it to his face and those mesmerizing chocolate eyes, and claims my mouth as his and only his.

Each time our mouths touch, a spark grows higher and higher, and before I can keep myself in check, it's a full out fire burning between us. My hands are all over him, and he is all over me as well, until there is a tap at the door. We stop, and our breath is short. Piper and Tessa enter.

"Sorry, y'all, but Tessa just got a call from Dustin. He overheard Dylan talking to Trent tonight."

The heat that I just felt running through my veins from Cash has just been replaced by ice. I know this isn't good.

"What did he say, Sis?"

I can see that she is struggling for words. "He said he heard Dylan tell Trent that it wouldn't be long until he had you. He didn't know if he was just bragging, but with that track record, he didn't want to risk not letting you know."

"Thanks, Sis. I know things are going to have to heat up between us, and it makes me nauseous. He will not have that piece of me ever again."

Cash pulls me in close as Piper and Tessa wait for what I'm going to say next.

"Aight, it's time for me to really tell you the plan and make it foolproof." They nod, and we sit in the floor.

"First off, this is going to get hard for all of us. This week has shown me how much I truly hate him, what he did, and why we have to save every other girl from him. So, here's how it is going to work. I'm going to continue to act like I'm totally falling for Dylan. Y'all, he might be at my parents' Christmas party. Cash, are you going to be able to handle that?" He nods. "I'm going to play the perfect girlfriend. My remainder of the time here will be about practice, Christmas with my family, hanging out with Piper, and seeing if the Kluft girls are willing to celebrate New Year's here in the big metropolis of Grassy Pond. I'm sure there's going to be a party at the McCracken's. This way we can all be there, show the girls how we do it in the South, and we have backup for Dylan. If I can get him where I want him, then I'll take it to the police before I leave for break, but if not, I'm going to continue to use the Kluft girls and Joe while I'm at Southern. I'd really love to take him down where it would hurt the most... Southern States."

Piper looks at Cash and Tessa, and I do the same. Their faces are all blank. It's almost as if they are trying to process what I just said.

"Y'all? Are you okay?" I ask.

Cash stands, and I'm afraid he's leaving. Instead, he walks back and forth before he speaks, "Char-coal, I'm with ya, but I'm gonna need someone to help keep me sane. I have no clue who that is going to be because of the act we are all playing."

"Cash, I got ya, honey! Piper isn't gonna leave you out in the cold," Piper says as she links her arm through his. "Dylan knows that we still talk, so we're good. I might not be with you every second, but if you need me, you find me, no questions asked."

All our emotions are running high, and I'm exhausted. I can't let Cash leave like this. Hell, I don't want him to leave period. My phone buzzes, interrupting my thoughts.

Dylan: I hope u r thinking of me like I am of u! C u @pool in am.

Me: Of course I am! C u soon!

I hit the *Lock* button on my phone as fast as possible and toss it onto the bed. I want to escape the nightmare I am living, and I want to do that safe in the arms of Cash Money.

Without one word, Cash walks to me, pulls me in close, and holds me tight.

"Char-coal, I need to go." I shake my head no and tears start to fall effortlessly. "Shhh, don't cry. I'll see you tomorrow. I promise. I'll be with you until the end and forever. Remember?" I answer with my eyes, and his lips take away all the fears, questions, and unknown. I can't wait until this is over, and I'm finally able to shout to the rooftop how much I love my Cash Money.

Cash steps away and makes his way to the window. "Hey, can't I at least drive you to the club?" I ask.

"No, Char-coal, I need to walk alone."

That stung just a little, but I know that he needs some space to sort through everything.

As he swings his legs out the window, I walk to him. "Hey, Cash Money, I love you forever and ever."

"I know, Char-coal, and I can't wait until it's no longer hidden because I'm going to put you up on a pedestal for everyone to see how much I treasure you. Don't think I don't want you to go with me; I'd just hate if your dad caught us because then we'd have a big ol' kink in this plan." That warms my heart, and I give him a quick kiss before he vanishes into the night.

Once he's out of sight, here come Piper and Tessa.

"Dang, Char, I didn't know y'all were that serious. I mean, I think I knew, but it's totally obvious," Piper says. "I don't know how he's gonna keep it together."

"Pipe, you have to help him. That's the only way he's going to make it. Now, let's get some sleep. That pool is going to call my name way too early in the morning."

"Night, y'all," Tessa says as she goes to her room, and Piper and I fall asleep instantly only to be awakened by that awful alarm clock.

Chapter 17

I slam my hand on top of the alarm and hit the *Snooze* button one time. Ten minutes later, it goes off again, and I slowly roll out of the bed. Piper covers her head with the blanket and mumbles something about being here when I get back.

I grab my bag, slowly make my way downstairs, and grab a piece of bacon on the way out the door. "Thanks," I tell Mama as I leave.

The parking lot is starting to get fuller since the first day I got back. This means more people to put between Dylan and me.

Grabbing my bag, I close the door and follow the same routine as I have since I was seven. Get up and swim my ass off. I eat, sleep, and breathe it. There is only one thing that I desire more, and that's Cash Money. The smell of chlorine hits my nostrils, and I'm awake and ready for the workout that is waiting.

Dylan is in lane two in the middle of a set. I quickly make my way to the locker room, change, grab the workout, and dive in lane one.

Before Dylan starts his next set, he waits on me. His perfectly chiseled chest is perched on the lane rope like he is King of GPAC.

"Mornin', Char. Just so you know, thoughts of you kept me up all night."

"Give me a break, Dylan. You know that's not the case," I say as I perch myself against the gutter in lane one.

"Char, you are always in my thoughts, and if everyone wasn't around, I'd show you exactly what I mean."

"I bet." I adjust my goggles and start my next set.

After twenty more minutes, our workouts are over, and Dylan hangs around to help me out of the pool, even though I don't need it.

We separate at the locker room, but not before Dylan kisses me briefly on the cheek. I glance back at him as I make my way to shower, change, and hurry so I can meet Piper.

"So, I'll see you later tonight," Dylan informs me as he walks me to my car.

"Aight, is it another double date?"

"That's a negative. It's just us."

"Okay," I almost stutter.

"Char, I'm not gonna make you do anything you don't want to. I promise."

"What are we going to do?"

"I was thinking about taking you to see the new movie, ya know, from that book. What's it called?"

"*The Hobbit?*"

"Yeah, I think so. I know you like to read and all."

"Um, yeah, but I like a good book with a great book boyfriend, and that's not one. How about that Madea Christmas one? I just wanna laugh, and that's a guarantee."

"Whatever. You wanna go eat somewhere nicer than the Burger Shak, especially since we are going to the city anyways?"

"Sure, what about Texas Roadhouse?"

"That sounds really good actually. I'll pick you up at five thirty." He captures my lips once more before closing the car door and walking to the Mustang.

I crank up the Honda, blast the heat, crank up some Florida Georgia Line to lighten my mood, and make my way to wake up Piper.

Dad is up early as usual and out at the barn. He waves to me when I get out of the car, and I hurry up the steps to the house.

Piper, Tessa, and Mama are in the kitchen eating breakfast.

"I'm glad Sleeping Beauty decided to wake up," I say as I steal a piece of bacon from Piper's plate.

"Hey now! Get your own!" she says as she smacks my hand. I shrug it off and do exactly that. I pile my plate full of grits, bacon, eggs, and homemade biscuits.

"Hungry, Char?" Tessa asks.

"I worked up an appetite. Y'all know what it's like when you swim. It's like all that water just makes you want to eat and sleep for days."

"So, how did things go last night, girls?" Mama asks.

"Good, I guess. I'm going to the movies in the city with Dylan tonight."

"Don't you think y'all are moving a little fast? I mean, I just don't want you to forget who you are. Sometimes we women need to learn to be without a guy."

Tessa, Piper, and I all stop and listen because we know there is a story that is getting ready to be told, and it will be one that teaches a lesson. One that I'm sure I need to hear.

"Girls, before your dad and I got together forever, I had bounced from one guy to another."

Tessa interrupts, "So, Mama, were you a hoochie mama? Because if so, ewwww, I don't want to hear anymore!"

"No, ma'am, I was not! In fact, that's why I never settled down. I didn't put out!"

Piper, Tessa, and I look at each other and our hands fly over our mouths. She has no filter, ever!

"Now, some of my friends did, but me, no. Your grandma would have shot the guy and me! Anyways, one day your grandma had to put in her two cents. Each time she'd give me a lecture, I'd run straight into another guy's arms, but I didn't put out. During my junior year, I was at the Burger Shak and your father walked in. We had known each other forever. He had lots of girls after him, and he decided to pull up a seat beside me. He was different. He wasn't about wooing me; instead, he wanted to be my friend. That friendship grew into the best love possible. I spent an entire year off at college without a boyfriend, and it was the best thing I had ever done. Your father did the same. When we came home after freshman year, we both knew who we were as individuals and there was no doubt that our friendship was the foundation for the relationship that was destined to bloom. We also knew that becoming a couple could change things if they didn't work out, but the moment he took me fishing for our first date and then his lips touched mine, I was his hook, line, and sinker! Girls, just thinkin' about it gets me tore up!"

"Mama! Stop! I don't want to hear anything else! Yuck!" I say.

"Come on, Mama. I wanna know more," Tessa says. Of course, she does. She always wants to know all the juicy details and then give a play-by-play later.

"Mama Number Two, I knew you and Pops were hot stuff back in the day!" Piper adds.

"I don't know about y'all, but it's getting hot in this kitchen, and I need to get outta here," I say as I put my plate into the sink. Tessa and Piper follow suit while Mama sits there smiling and drinkin' her coffee.

About that time, Dad walks into the room, and we snicker.

"What was that about?" he asks Mama.

"Let's just say that I let them in on how things were we when we were young and foolish," she says as she stands and moves toward Dad and places her arms around his neck.

"On that note, we are definitely out," Tessa says as she makes kissy faces as she passes them.

The fact that my parents are as in love as they were twenty-five years ago makes me proud. I can honestly say that will be Cash and me one day. I'm sure of it. It's just gonna take a little time to get Dylan completely out of the picture.

We all make our way to my bedroom, and that's when the questions start. Where are we going? What time am I leaving? How am I gonna let them know what's going on? What will I do if he tries something? They keep going on and on.

"Y'all stop! I'll be fine. I just need you to know where I am and when I should be home. If I'm not, then you need to worry. He was almost apologetic at practice. If he's on his game, then he won't try anything tonight. It will be later. He needs to know that he has me for sure."

I take out my phone and text Cash. As always, he calls me before he replies. I explain the same thing to him, and he calms down. I also promise him that he will be who I'm with at the end of the night. We disconnect, and I return my attention to Piper and Tessa who are picking out my outfit for tonight.

They've done a pretty good job. Glancing at my bed, I see a pair of Miss Me Jeans, a V-neck long-sleeved red shirt with a lace camisole to go underneath, and my boots.

"Good job, ladies!"

"Well, you know you have to look the part," Tessa says.

"True dat!" I say.

"Uh, please don't talk like that again," Piper states. "That in a redneck Southern drawl isn't cute." She pauses. "Well, I guess I better get home. I think Mom wants to get the decorations finished, and everybody has to be there. Let me know when you get home and if you need me tonight."

"I will," I reply. Piper gives me a hug and heads home. Tessa and I decide to go out on the farm and see what all the animals are up to.

We walk out the back door and get on the Gator. We start at the back of the farm and make our way up. Dad is in the shed working on the tractor. We stop by to see if there is anything he needs us to do. He just says for us to make sure the goats are still near the pond. We are on it, and it also gives me a reason to get close to Cash's farm.

We follow the perimeter of the farm toward the pond. Tessa and I don't say much until we realize that Joker, along with his two siblings, has jumped the damn fence again.

"Oh my gosh, Char! How are we going to get them back across?"

"Easy. Pick up their asses, unless they decide to be as stubborn as usual."

"That's so not funny. You think Cash can help us, or is that off limits, too?"

"I'm okay with him helping if he's outside. You see him anywhere?"

We both look around, but we don't see him.

"Tess, let's just try it, okay?"

I put the Gator in park, and we try to call them back across, which is a negative. Joker and I have our own way with words. Pretty much I keep it blunt, pull on his horns, and he gets the picture. Slowly but surely, he makes it across. I just need Tessa to hold the fence, so he can cross.

Once he is back inside, we work on the others. One at a time, we get them across. After the last one is back on our property, I see Cash in the distance. He looks our way almost like he's unsure of how to react. Then, I watch him walk away. My heart breaks to see him act like we are nothing, even if it is an act.

"Charley, he's only doing what he has to and what you asked him to do."

"I know, but it doesn't make it any easier. Let's make our way back to the house. I'm gonna need another shower after all this mess."

"Whatever, I could use a cup of Mama's hot chocolate."

On the way back to the Gator, something creeps into my brain. I feel a pull toward the club. I need to go up there for some reason.

"Tessa, can we check out the club? I just feel like I need to go up there."

"Sure, you want me to hang out down here or come up with ya?"

"I think I'll be all right. It could be nothin'."

Making my way to the ladder, I look back to where Cash was standing, only to find he's no longer there. Then, I see him sitting on the bench outside his barn, like he's waiting. I hurry up the ladder and look around the club. It doesn't take me long to notice what's different.

There is something carved into the wood below the window and overlooking the pond. I walk closer, squat down, and run my fingers across it.

Char-Coal + $ = 4ever & ever

My heart warms, and it amazes me how in tune Cash and I are. I pull out my prepaid phone and text him.

Me: 4ever & ever & ever. I Love U $!

Cash: U like?

Me: I <3 TY!

Cash: Meet me there tonight.

Me: K

"Hey, Char, everything okay up there?"

"Yeah, you gotta see this. Come here."

Tessa comes up the stairs and looks around, trying to figure out what is different. It takes her a good five minutes to notice, but when she does, her smile lights up the room.

"Char, I wouldn't have even noticed it because it blends in perfectly with the wood and location. Can you imagine when y'all's kids come here to play?"

"Um, I don't know about all that. This is our spot, ya know? But I guess you're right. It would be neat for our kids to experience this. I mean, the club, farm, country life, getting your hands dirty, and keeping things simple."

Tessa and I make our way out of the club and back to the barn. We return the Gator and spend a few minutes with Dad in the barn. He's cleaning the horses' hooves. I join in and help, and Tessa watches as usual. It's nice to spend some quality time with Dad.

"Char, with practice you haven't been able to get in a tree, have ya?"

"Nope, but I'm hoping I can a couple of days before the season goes out."

"You got *the one* and now are takin' it easy. It's okay. You got the Big Buck Contest in the bag this year."

"Maybe."

I finish helping Dad, and then we head to the house. I'm about to starve, but I don't want to eat too much since I'm going to eat with Dylan.

Mama has a crockpot of chili beans going. Tessa and I each grab a cup and get comfortable on the couch. Mama is watching a rerun of *Mama's Family*, and we watch it with her.

"Is the chili good, girls?"

"Yes, ma'am," we say on cue.

After eating just a little, I excuse myself and get ready for my date with Dylan. I take my time because not only do I need to look the part, but I'm also worried about being alone. I don't believe anything will happen tonight, but who's to say that won't happen. I know a few things though. I will not leave my drinks unattended, and I will keep up my guard.

Turning on the radio, I try to focus on anything but what is about to occur. That is until Luke Bryan comes on the radio. "Crash My Party" echoes through the speakers, and that song means more to me than words can express. Not only is that Cash Money's ringtone, but I also know without any doubt that if I call Cash, he will come to my rescue. He doesn't care what he's doing, where he is, or what he will lose in the process, and that means more to me than life itself. I stop to stare in the mirror and reflect on my plan. Does it reflect those same feelings for Cash? Or, am I being selfish because I want to hurt Dylan like he hurt me? Either way, I don't like who I see in this reflection, and I want this to be over sooner rather than later.

When the song changes to a more upbeat one by Taylor Swift, I pull myself from those thoughts and finish getting ready. As I'm adding the final accessories to my wardrobe, I hear Mama call that Dylan is here. I grab my purse, coat, and head downstairs. Dylan is standing there in a pair of AE jeans, a fitted vintage style long-sleeved tee, and a pair of Sanuks.

What catches me off guard is the bouquet of blue roses in his hand. *That's different. I wonder what they symbolize.* I take them from him and thank him with a kiss on the cheek. Then, I turn to Mama who takes them from me, and we make our way to the car.

Dylan guides me to the car with his hand on the small of my back. Again, he plays the perfect gentleman role to a T by opening the car door, asking if I'm comfortable, what

I want to listen to on the radio, and so on. The only thing I want right now is to be out of this car, but instead, I make the best of it and ask for a little country because Dylan hates country music. That in itself should have been clue number one for me to stay away from him.

He does as I wish and the night gets a little better when it's like the big man upstairs is looking out for me as Florida Georgia Line comes on.

"Did you know there's a remix of this on the other stations with Nelly?" Dylan asks.

"Yeah, but the original is way better. They are going places fast, and I can say I used to listen to them before people had a clue about them."

"You're right about that. I thought if I had to hear "Cruise" one more time I was going to break your damn iPod."

"Dylan Sloan, you wouldn't dare!"

"No, I wouldn't, but seriously, who's gonna be the next big thing, if you had to guess?"

"That's easy! Cole Swindell and then Chase Rice isn't far behind him!"

"I'm sure you're right. So, what's been your favorite thing about college?"

"Definitely the friends I've made. The Kluft girls are like my sisters. They helped me decide to swim again. I missed it so much. I think some of them might actually be coming to Grassy Pond for New Year's."

"What are they going to do here for New Year's?"

"You know as well as I do, there'll be a party somewhere. Hayden and Anna are about to die to meet some good ol' country boys."

"I bet."

Before I know it, we are at Texas Roadhouse and those cheese fries are calling my name. If I've got to be on a date with Dylan, I'm going to eat what I want. One thing that I've never been scared to do is eat in front of a guy. Now, the only problem is keeping it down.

Conversation at supper is easy and like it used to be before the incident. I try to focus on that time when we were happy, or at least, I thought we were.

Once supper is finished, we make our way to the theater. Dylan offers to buy popcorn and drinks, but I'm stuffed. He gets a drink, and I know I'm safe tonight because he doesn't offer me an extra straw or anything. I'll just drink straight out of his since there is no way he's going to poison himself.

The movie is hilarious, and at one point, I'm crying I'm laughing so hard. When it ends, we make our way back to Grassy Pond. Dylan doesn't push himself on me; he walks me to the front door, kisses me on the cheek, and turns to walk away. *Odd.*

"Thanks for a great night," I say.

He stops and turns around on the step. "Charley, I meant what I said when I told you I was sorry about before. I'm not that person anymore," he says it with no hint of lying in his eyes, but I know better.

"I'm glad. I'll talk to you tomorrow sometime after church. I'm taking a day off from the pool."

"Okay, night."

Walking inside, I hang my coat on the hook and make sure the door is locked. I'm in earlier than midnight, and my family is up playing Uno in the kitchen.

"Can I play?"

"Sure, as soon as I beat their butts," Tessa says.

"Let's just see about that," Dad replies.

"Well, while y'all finish this round, I'm going to change. I'll be right back."

Hurrying upstairs, I text Piper that I'm home and fine. She informs me that she's been talking to Joe all night, and he wants to visit her before she goes back to school. Then, I call Cash because I just need to hear his voice.

"Hey, Char-coal."

"Hey, Cash Money, it's so good to hear your voice."

"I've been waiting all night to hear yours as well. Do I need to head toward the club?"

"Give me just a little bit. Mama, Dad, and Tessa are playing Uno downstairs, and I wanna whoop their butts real quick. I have a feeling Mama and Dad are ready to call it a night. Once they are in their room, I'll text ya."

"Sounds good. I'll see you soon. Love you."

"Love you, too." After we hang up, I change and hurry downstairs for a family fun game of Uno.

I make my way to the fridge for a Choice Cherry Gold and take a seat beside Tessa. "She beat ya, huh?"

"Like always. I swear she cheats," Dad says.

"I do not!"

"Let's deal and see who wins this time," I say as I push my shoulder into Tessa's.

"Hey now!"

The next thirty minutes is Rice family time, and it's perfect. There are so many memories attached to nights like these when I was younger, and Tessa always won or made you feel bad if she didn't. She beats me, but mainly because I have other plans tonight.

Mama and Dad retire to their room, and Tessa and I hang out in the kitchen, putting away the cards and snacks.

"Soooooo, how was it tonight?"

"Okay, actually. He didn't try anything. That was kinda weird or not like him. He even apologized again. Oh, and those flowers? Totally not like him. I've gotta figure out what that color represents."

"No worries. I did that already. They are beautiful, but who buys blue roses?"

"What do they mean?"

Tessa doesn't say anything; instead, she pulls out her iPhone and opens Safari. She hands it to me, and I read, "The unattainable, the impossible." I stop, stare, and think about those words. What is he trying to imply? Am I the impossible, or is my goal of escaping him unattainable?

Chapter 18

I hand Tessa back her phone without saying a word. I push the meaning to the back of my mind. She searches for what to say, but elects to give me a hug instead as she whispers that it's going to be all right into my ear.

I pull away and take out my prepaid phone and text Cash. Tessa knows where I am going, but she doesn't want me to go alone. I agree to have Cash meet me at the barn.

Tessa watches me walk to the barn from the back porch, and Cash and I make our way to the club.

We don't talk for the first hour. He just holds me in his arms as we dance to the music on the radio. If only time could freeze, and I never had to face another day with Dylan, life would be perfect.

Eventually, Cash whispers into my ear that we need to talk about what's in our near future. It kinda catches me off guard. I thought I was his future.

We take a seat on the futon, and Cash explains.

"Char, we have a lot going on in the next two weeks before you go back to Southern. We need to have a plan for every event."

I look at him like I'm lost because I am.

"Tomorrow at church, do we have a plan? Your parents' Christmas party, do we have a plan? New Year's? You see what I mean?"

"Yeah, I see what you mean. What are you thinking?"

"I'm thinking that I'm going to be ready to beat Dylan's ass if I have to watch you two at these places."

I take Cash's hand in mine. "Look, Cash. There is no need to worry at church because we will sit with our parents. The others might be difficult, but I'm thinking the Kluft girls can help with New Year's."

"Aight, I'm listenin'."

"My parents' Christmas party is Christmas Eve. That one is gonna be tough, but it can be doable. Just remember that I'll meet you here later to exchange our presents, okay?"

"Okay, but what about New Year's?"

"Hayden and Anna are all about finding a country boy since they met you. I figured they could help run an interference, along with Caroline, Tori, Sarah, and Georgia. I plan to call them tomorrow, but I do think you need a date to Mama and Dad's party, as much as I hate to say that."

"No way! I'm not going with someone else. Besides, who would go with me?"

"What about Sally?"

"No! I'm not going with anyone. I'll just make an appearance and try to stay clear of him."

"Piper?"

"No, Char-coal."

"Well, if you feel like that would be better for you, then do it. Plus, it might make it look more realistic."

"No, it won't. If I want you to move home and not go back to school, there is no way I'm moving on to someone else that quickly."

"Okay, you have a point. Can we quit talking about this?"

"Sure." I make him forget everything around us by kissing his lips long and hard. He begins to lose that thought and lose himself in me.

Before we know it, Cash is on top of me, and we have our hands in places that our parents would kill us over.

Cash continues to stay true to his word, and he pulls away from me so things don't go any further.

"Ya know what I wanted to do this year for New Year's?" he asks.

I shake my head no.

"I wanted to take you somewhere you've never been, but have always wanted to go."

My mind starts to race with all the possibilities, but only one stands out in my mind. "Can I guess?" He nods. "Nashville."

"Ding, ding, ding. You are correct."

"Cash, that would cost a fortune. I can only imagine what Music City is like. One day we are going, that's for sure! And, when we do, I want to be the biggest tourist around!"

"Whatever your country heart desires."

We spend a little more time together before Cash takes me back to the house. Once we reach the barn, he kisses me like his life depends on it to breathe. I walk backwards to the house so that I can keep my eyes on the one that matters the most. I wave bye when I enter the back door and sneak upstairs.

Chapter 19

The next morning I'm woke up with Mama yelling for me to get up and get ready for church. I grumble, pull the covers above my head, and then jump up because I know for the next two hours I get to see my Cash Money. Even if we can't talk, we are going to be in the same room.

Since I'm moving a little slower this morning, Mama and Dad go on to Sunday school, and Tessa waits behind with me.

We arrive for Sunday school ten minutes late, and I'm relieved to know that Dylan isn't here this morning. My heart also skips a beat when I see Cash sitting across the room.

The lesson is exactly what I needed to hear, and we make our way to preaching. Cash's family is directly behind me with the Sloan's to my right. *Talk about uncomfortable!* Piper is two rows ahead of us.

By 11:55, people are beginning to get restless, and the preacher wraps up the sermon. Once the closing hymn and benediction are finished, we walk outside. Cash doesn't hang around, and he is heading down the main road by the time I make it down the front steps of the church.

I wait on Dylan to see what his plans are for the rest of the day and the week. We decide to see each other tomorrow at the pool. He knows that this week is busy with practice, the Christmas party, Christmas Day, and spending time with our families. He walks me to the car, kisses me goodbye, and Dustin does the same with Tessa.

We make our way home for a fabulous home-cooked Sunday lunch, complete with country style steak, homemade mashed potatoes, corn, green beans, and rolls.

Now that I'm as full as a tick, I relax for the remainder of the afternoon. Tessa and I enjoy a little sister time, and then Piper comes over to join in the Christmas movie marathon. I text Cash and let him know we are taking it easy today, and I'll talk to him later tonight.

I don't think about Dylan, the plan, or anything except a perfect afternoon with two of my favorite girls in the world.

As the night arrives, Piper goes home because I have to go to practice in the morning. Dylan calls to see how my day has been, and Tessa decides to sleep in my room with me.

As I doze off, I hear a tapping at the window, and I don't need to think about who it is. That is until I realize it's not Cash; it's Dylan.

"What are you doin' here?" I say with my arms crossed in front of my body.

"I just wanted to surprise you and give you a goodnight kiss." At the same time Dylan speaks, Tessa moves, causing him to look confused.

"It's Tessa." She wipes her eyes and does a double take. Then, she waves and lies back down.

"Sorry, if I'd have known you weren't alone, I would have stayed home."

"It's all right. Come here." I pull him by his shirt and kiss his lips. "Now, go before my parents wake up! I'll see you in the morning."

"Okay, okay. I'll see you in the morning." He kisses me again and makes his way back out of the window.

I shut it and lock it. Crawling back into bed, I hear my door creak open. "Char, is everything okay? I thought I heard a guy's voice."

"Yeah, we're fine. Tessa's stayin' in here tonight."

"Oh, okay. Sleep tight. Love y'all."

"Night, love you, too." She closes the door, and we both exhale loudly.

Tessa whispers, "Ohmygawsh that was close, and what the hell was that? Has he done that before?"

"No, he hasn't. Oh no! What if he saw Cash do that the other night? What if he's in trouble?"

"Don't worry. He's gone. I'll text Cash real quick though."

Tessa texts Cash to tell him to keep his eyes and ears open. He feels like there is no need to worry, but we decide not to meet up until Christmas Eve.

Eventually, I doze off, and of course, awakened by that awful alarm clock. *Seriously?!*

Chapter 20

Monday through Thursday is exactly the same. I wake up, go to practice, get ready, eat lunch with Dylan, help Mama and Dad at the house and farm, eat supper, and repeat until Christmas Eve.

I wake up Christmas Eve and stare at the clock. It's 10:30. When was the last time I saw that? I don't have practice; it's just time to celebrate the reason for the season. I grab my phone and notice I have four missed texts, one from Piper, two from Dylan, and one from Georgia. Glancing at them, I decide to check Georgia's first.

Georgia: Miss ya bunches! We still getting together?

I don't reply; I just hit *Call.*

"About time, Char! I figured you were at the pool, but it wasn't that long of a set today." She takes a breath before realizing I'm still half asleep.

"Yeah, well, I decided to sleep in. I haven't missed a day yet. I was planning on calling you to see about your plans for New Year's, because um…" I pause. I don't know how I'm going to explain all of this to her. "I'm kinda seeing Dylan… like a lot."

She wastes no time before she butts in. "What the hell, Char? This better be good because he is a piece of shit. Please tell me you didn't fall for his crap! Wait. What is Cash saying about this? I mean, I don't even know what to say! Where is my strong Charley who's ready to kick some ass and take some names?"

"Georgia, hold up. Don't get too excited. I can explain."

"You better."

"When I got home, I decided I needed to put a stop to this, but on my own terms. I want Dylan Sloan to suffer, pay for what he did, and in doing that, I'm making him trust me. Then, when he's completely oblivious, I'm taking him to the big house."

"And, how are you going to do that? He's dangerous. Don't get yourself in over your head."

"Listen, Georgia. I have it all figured out, but I need your help along with the rest of the Kluft girls. I was thinkin' it's 'bout time to show those Yankees how we do it in the South. Whatcha think?"

"Hell yeah! Hayden and Anna will die! 'Cause you know we're outstanding in our field!"

"Damn right, we are! So, let's say y'all come up on that Thursday, and we can all practice together New Year's Eve at GPAC. Anna and Hayden can hang out with Piper and Tessa."

"Speakin' of Piper, what in the heck has happened with her and Joe with all the shit that's gone down?"

"Well… you're not gonna believe this, but Joe did what he had to do in order to protect me. Dylan was at Whiskey River that night. Joe knew if I went, there was no telling what Dylan would have done to me."

"Char, are you kidding? I never would have thought that. I mean, I didn't want to think he was as bad as Dylan, but he really didn't give us any reason to believe that he was on our side. It looked really bad!"

"I know, and I basically got in a big argument with Piper about it. She told me she talked to him, and I pretty much lost it on her. Then, my eyes were opened, and we are all good now."

"Speaking of being all good with people, how's Cash? Is he okay with this?"

"No, he's not, but he agrees we had to do something. He doesn't like my plan, but knows that I'm only going to do things my way. Tonight's gonna be rough though, because we have to go to my parents' Christmas party, and Dylan's my date."

"Shut the front door! Char, that's awful! Please tell me Cash has a date."

"He refused to bring anyone. He thought that might make it look more real since he's playing this overprotective lover role. I'm just hoping he doesn't beat Dylan's ass if he touches me."

"Char, what are you going to do about that? You know he's gonna expect some type of action."

"He's been a gentleman so far except the fact that I need a gallon of hand sanitizer when he touches me."

"I think I just threw up in my mouth! Yuck! Please tell me you're not gonna let it go far."

"I promise I'm not. That's why I need y'all to run an interference at the New Year's Eve party."

"I'll call all the Kluft girls and see if they are in for New Year's. I'm sure they will, but Char, stay safe. I can't wait to see you. Have a Merry Christmas."

I hang up with Georgia and call Piper. We are meeting for a last minute shopping trip to get something festive for tonight's party. Then, I look at Dylan's text.

Dylan: I've dreamt of you all night again & missed u at GPAC this morning.

Dylan: my lips missed yours 2.

Oh my gosh! I really think I'm gonna be sick. I grab my sanitizer from the bedside table and wash off my hands and wipe down my cell phone. Not like it's gonna do anything since it was just a text, but it still gave me the creeps. It's the first time I've seen him say or type something that bold since this charade started.

I shake the thought from my head and gather my things to shower and get ready for the mad dash to Northlake with Piper.

As I'm drying my hair, Tessa comes into the bathroom and almost scares me to death.

"Don't do that shit, Tess!"

"Sorry, I just wanted you to know I talked to Cash this morning." My mood suddenly changes, and I feel a happiness that I've lacked since I woke up.

"What'd he say?"

With a huge grin, she acts like it's a big secret. "Spit it out, Tess!"

"He said that he can't wait to see you tonight, and he will be on his best behavior. Oh, he also said something about meeting him later. I don't really remember those details." She giggles, knowing that was the most important part. I take my comb and chunk it at her. She ducks and begins to laugh harder. I cut my eyes at her, and she knows I'm done with the conversation if she doesn't have the info I want to hear.

"Hey, Tessa, do you wanna go shopping with us today?"

"Heck yeah! Can I see if Sally wants to go, too?"

"It's fine by me, but that means we have to be careful what we say."

"Never mind then because we have got to talk about tonight."

I finish getting ready, and we talk to Mama until Piper arrives. We load up in Piper's car and make our way to Northlake. Traffic is horrible. What were we thinking? It's Christmas Eve.

"Y'all, can we like rethink this plan? Traffic is insane!" Piper says.

I look at Tessa, and we both raise our shoulders. I just need a dress that screams Charley, something in which Dylan would approve, but more importantly, Cash will love later tonight. This could be difficult.

"Hey, since we're close to Lebo's, can we just check there?" I ask.

Piper and Tessa look at me like I have got to be kidding.

"Char, we could have gone to the damn General Store for that!"

With a pouty lip, I reply, "Not really. Lebo's has so much more, and if there's nothing there, then we can hit up TJ Maxx."

That brings a smile to their faces, and we are at Lebo's in no time. I walk inside and glace at the women's clothing. I see it. I know exactly what dress I need, but that might mean a new pair of boots in my future as well.

To my right is a black sequined zebra print dress with an asymmetrical hem, cap sleeves, and a scoop neck. It's perfect. I just hope they have my size.

Rustling through the rack, I find my size and hurry to the dressing room. As I make my way there, I notice a pair of Corral crystal inlay boots that are a perfect match with this dress. Glancing down the shelf, I find a size eight, grab them and take everything into the dressing room.

I slide on the dress. It's light, hugs at the right spots, and is just enough for the party. Slipping on the boots, I look into the mirror and know without a doubt that this is the outfit.

"Char, hurry up! Let's see it!" Tessa exclaims from outside the dressing room.

As I open the door, Tessa's mouth drops, and Piper squeals like I've found the perfect prom dress or something.

"Char, Cash is gonna fall out when he sees you!"

Tessa speaks her mind, "More like be ready to take her out of that dress."

I place my hands on my hips and give Tessa the look. I turn around to change, but before I do, I look into the mirror one last time. Cash is going to love it! The boots totally set it off, and Dylan will approve, too.

I hurry to dress, pay, and cringe at the total as I pass my debit card to the clerk. The clerk laughs as she swipes it and gives it back. I take my card, place it back into my wallet and we head toward the door.

We make our way to TJ Maxx, find Tessa and Piper new outfits for tonight, and then return to Grassy Pond.

"So, Charley, what'd you get Cash for Christmas?"

"Actually, it's kinda something for both of us."

"Whatcha mean?"

"I got two tickets to see Florida Georgia Line in February."

Tessa bursts out in song while pushing down the power windows. "Baby you a song, you make me wanna roll my windows down and cruise."

"Roll up that damn window! It's freakin' cold in here!" Piper exclaims.

I smile. I love these two, and they have been here every step of the way. "Yeah, I thought it would be fun, but now I'm worried 'cause what if all this mess isn't over by then?"

"He can take me instead," Tessa states with a straight face.

"You wouldn't dare!"

"Hey, no need to miss out on a good country boy in action."

"Oh, I'll be going. No worries. I pray this shit with Dylan is over by then."

"Speakin' of Dylan," Piper pipes in, "what's the deal with tonight?"

"Okay, the party starts at seven thirty. Dylan is coming around eight. That gives us a little time to get ourselves together. Plus, that way Cash will hopefully get to see me first."

"Sis, you know that's gonna be a problem. Cash is one that is going to wear his emotions on his sleeves. You know his parents will get there earlier, and he will be with them. I just pray y'all can have a moment alone before the other guests arrive."

"That would be fabulous. I just need him to hold me for a minute." Tessa and Piper glance at each other. "What? I do! There is just something about those arms. I feel lost without him. I just keep telling myself this is all worth it."

"Char, it will be, and I can't wait for that asshole Dylan to rot in hell. I wish Joe could have come down, but that would look too suspicious. I thought about inviting him for New Year's. What do y'all think about that?"

"I'd love for him to be here because I do need to apologize, but how do you think that will play in with Dylan?" I ask.

"Joe's been trying to play in with our game as well. He's trying to get back on Dylan's good side, or at least let him know that you and Cash are finished."

Those words sting as I hear Piper say them. I never want us to be finished. When that happens, it will be when one of us leaves this world. Until then, Cash Money is mine forever and ever.

As we hit the Grassy Pond city limits, we make a few last minute plans before we get to the farm and stop by Piper's house to grab a few things for tonight because she's staying.

When we arrive back at the farm, the sun is starting to set. Mama has already turned on all the Christmas lights in the house, and the large pine is lit up like the tree at Rockefeller Center in New York City.

We hurry inside the house and check to see what my parents are up to. Dad is helping Mama finish the food in the kitchen and looks all spiffed up. No longer is he wearing his dirty Carhartts, thermal shirt, and boots; he's in a pair of "dressy" Carhartts with a solid button-up shirt. I have to say that he does clean up nicely. One thing he won't do without is his camo ball cap. It's his trademark, just like my boots. My heart warms as I watch them work together, not realizing that they have an audience.

"Hey, girls! Y'all look like you bought out the store," Mama says.

"Charley, is that a Lebo's bag, young lady?" Dad scowls.

"Yes, Dad, but I had to have this dress."

"I'm not worried about the dress; I'm worried about the price tag on the boots! Did you use my credit card for emergencies only?"

"No, sir. In fact, I used my debit card."

Mama tries to hide a smile and laugh. "Hun, you do know we're paying for it regardless."

"Well, who's to stand between a girl and her new pair of boots?"

I run up and hug my dad. "Thanks!"

Tessa looks at Piper. "Dang, if I'd known that, I'd have bought out TJ Maxx!"

We go to my room and take turns showering while singing our hearts out to our local country station that is now playing Christmas music. There's something about anything Christmas that will put you in a good mood no matter what is going on.

"Y'all, we have got to listen to this CD! It's like classic Christmas!" Piper says like a giddy child. I look at her and see that it's Mariah Carey's *Merry Christmas* album. She's right. It's a classic and just keeps getting better and better.

About song number four, Mama knocks on the door to make sure that we are going to be ready before people arrive. As she is about to close the door, I hear her welcome Cash's mom. I smile, knowing he's downstairs, but I have to pretend like I don't. I close my eyes, take a deep breath, and focus on the task at hand. Taking Dylan down.

When I open my eyes, Piper and Tessa are staring at me.

"Char, are you okay?"

"Yeah, this is just gonna be hard, Tessa. All I really wanna do is run into those arms, but knowing that I have to act otherwise is tearing me up inside."

"Well, I tell ya what. Tessa and I will go down first and get a feel for everything. Then, you make your entrance, and we will somehow find a way for Cash and you to be alone."

"Y'all are the best! I love y'all. You know that, right?"

They both envelop me in a hug before going downstairs. I pace back and forth while continuing to sing to the CD.

"Miss You Most at Christmas Time" bleeds through the speakers, and I feel the tears begin to build. I walk toward my bathroom because I can't cry, ruin my makeup, and be a hot mess. Instead, I need to hold the pieces together.

I grab a makeup sponge and begin to touch up my eyeliner, and as I move toward the mirror, I see the most beautiful eyes ever to cross mine. Cash.

As I turn to face him, his arms are already open. I wrap my arms around his neck and breathe in his strong scent. All the pinned-up emotion I've been holding in since last week wants to release, but I know if it does, it will be one big overflowing dam, so I decide to pull myself away.

"How'd you get up here?"

"Two of our favorite girls let me in on a secret. Something about me needing to see you first."

I feel bashful for the first time in a long time, almost as if it's Cash seeing me for who I really am.

"Don't do that, Char-coal. Move back and let me see why I had to see ya first."

Stepping back from Cash, I let go of his hand and back out of the bathroom. Once I'm a few feet from him, I stop and put my hands on my hips and wait for a response.

He looks me from head to toe with his smile growing wider and wider with each inch. I twirl for him to get the full effect.

Before I make the full 360 degrees, Cash has closed the distance. He takes my hand and pulls me into him, like we are dancing at the local country bar. He dips me back and lays the sweetest lips on Earth to mine.

He brings me back up, and I don't let go; instead, my lips devour his. I'm hungry for him, and I know that I have to make this end sooner than later.

"Char-coal, I gotta get back down there, or my parents are going to start wondering. If we're both missing, it's not gonna look the way we want it to. Meet me at the club tonight. Just have Tessa text me when you're on the way."

"Aight. Oh, and Cash Money, you look rather handsome tonight."

"Do I? Well, you'll have to tell me all about it later when I know we have time, just you and me."

He lifts my chin so our eyes meet and brushes his lips with mine before going back downstairs. I give Mariah one more song before I make my grand entrance. It's still early, so there is time to help Mama.

Making my way down the stairs, my nostrils are hit with Mama's famous hot chocolate, and I can hear everyone hurrying to get the last minute touches together. My hand glides down the railing as I listen to all the conversations.

I make my way to the kitchen to help Mama place the last of the food onto the dining room table. She has anything and everything you can imagine.

As I start to snatch one of her cheesecake bites, she smacks my hand. "Char, at least get one from the fridge. Don't mess up my platter."

"Sorry, Mama." I hurry back to the kitchen and round the corner and my breath hitches when I see Cash bent over a cooler. Hot damn! That ass is fine! I clear my throat. He glances over his shoulder and winks.

"Hey, Char, so Mama got you, too, huh?" Tessa questions when she sees me open the fridge.

"Yup, I mean, they're all gonna be gone off there within five minutes of the party starting."

"True, but you know Mama, she's gotta make sure it's just right when the first people arrive."

Cash makes his way out of the kitchen as we try and ignore each other. Tessa, Piper, and I hang out in the kitchen until the doorbell rings. Glancing at my watch, I know I still have a few minutes before Dylan arrives.

I'm just about to tell Tessa and Piper the plan for tonight when I see *him* in the doorway. Dylan is standing there in a pair of dark jeans that fall low on his hips and a flannel button-up shirt. If I didn't know better, I'd enjoy the view.

"Hey, Dylan," I say. I brush my dress down as I slide out of my seat and stand to meet him. His eyes do the same moves as Cash's, but it doesn't have the same effect. I pretend that it does though. I sway my hips as I walk toward him, wrap my arms around his neck and pull him in for a kiss. I whisper into his ear, "So, was that everything you dreamt about?"

With a loss of words, Dylan just uses his lips to talk. As my lips move, my brain is wishing they would get off me. While I try to figure out how I'm going to get out of this predicament, Tessa comes to the rescue.

"Get a room, you two! Where's Dustin?"

"Right here, Tess," Dustin says as he greets Tessa with open arms.

"Dang, I need a man!" Piper says.

When I pull away from him, he wraps his arm around my waist and kisses my cheek.

"Piper, you know Justin will be here later."

"That's not what I meant, Char."

"Oh."

Dylan looks at both of us and then gives a half-grin.

"She's got somebody in mind, but he's not my favorite person right now."

"Who would that be, Char?"

I cut my eyes at Dylan, "Seriously! That asshat, Joe, from Southern. Piper's got a thing for him, and he's full of complete shit!"

"Down, girl! He can't be that bad, can he? Maybe you just don't know everything?"

"Oh, and you do?" I scoff. "Oh, wait, you do. Don't you?" Everyone's eyes get wide as I talk.

"Charley, lower your voice," Dylan sneers as he grabs my arm tighter. This is the first sign of the old Dylan. "I told you I was sorry for all of that and I'm not the same person, but you've got to not bring it up. So what if she likes Joe? Let Piper have some fun. We all need to have some fun. Don't ya think?"

My insides are quivering, and I'm fuming. I really want to call this game quits now, but too much is at stake. I decide to play my cards right. I yank my arm from Dylan and storm out the back door. He follows just as I planned.

Stopping on the back porch, I turn to face him. "Dylan, I know you say you're sorry, but you don't know what he did to me. I trusted him, and he lied! I'm so stupid! I fell for some stupid guy again, and who's to say that you won't make me look that way again!"

Dylan looks caught off guard. Never in our previous relationship did I stand my ground when he questioned me.

"Look. Here I am with your ass again! Who's to say you won't go back to being the old Dylan, not the new and improved?"

Dylan almost stutters as he tries to find the right words. "Char, I'm not that guy anymore. I want to prove it to you. I want to show you how much you mean to me and what you have always meant to me. Please… please believe me," he says as he caresses my cheek.

Pulling everything from my inner core, I give it all I have and speak the most bullshit line I've ever said.

"I believe you, Dylan. I always knew you weren't that guy Trent made you become." I place my hand onto his chest and guide it up to the back of his neck as I gaze into his lying eyes. "Now, show me that what I believe is true."

He pulls his hand to grasp my neck and then leans toward me. He nibbles on my earlobe while trying to make me believe that he is truthful. I allow myself to let go, and my head falls backward. His body reacts, and I know he's falling right into my hands.

Chapter 21

"Charley, you know that dress is exactly what I'd hoped you'd wear. You look amazing."

"Thanks," I reply as I try to put out the fire that he is trying to build. "I think we need to get to the party. You know you still need to make my parents see you're different, ya know?"

"I guess you're right."

Dylan and I walk hand in hand into the house. People are gathered throughout mingling. All the parents are in the living room, and I want to make our presence known.

I guide Dylan into the living room to talk to his parents as well as mine.

"Hi, Mr. and Mrs. Sloan, how are you?"

"We're great, Charley. In fact, we are ecstatic to know you are both back on speaking terms."

"Yeah, I guess you could say that," Dylan says wryly. I just shake my head in agreement.

We make our way around the room and then to the family room where all the "kids" are hanging out. I see Piper, Tessa, Dustin, but where's Cash? My mind races, and I keep trying to figure out where he might be. Is he avoiding this? Is he really okay?

Just as the panic is about to take over, he walks into the room. His face looks rigid, almost like it's made of stone. I try to make eye contact, but it doesn't happen. Then, I turn to Dylan, and he just shrugs his shoulders like it's no big deal.

"Hey, Cash, no date tonight?" Dylan boasts.

"Nah."

"Well, too bad," he says as he pulls me tighter.

I look up at him and smile. We walk to the couch and sit near Tessa and Dustin. Cash does the best with what he has in the room. He talks to Sally. That stings a little, but I have no right to feel anything because what I'm doing to him must feel like a million stings.

Trying to take my mind off Cash, I glance around the room and see that Piper is talking to Justin as usual. I swear that's like her local boy toy. She just keeps him on a string for the hell of it.

We graze the food table multiple times, refill our hot chocolate, and sing Christmas carols. From the outside, this traditional Rice Christmas party looks normal, but in actuality, it is one big cluster.

Around eleven, the adults are tipsy and ready to go home. We have had our fun, and honestly, I'm tired from my charade. Cash excuses himself from his parents and us and makes his way home.

Once Cash leaves, Piper, Tessa, and I walk Justin, Dylan, and Dustin outside. We don't walk them to their cars; we say goodbye on the front porch.

Piper and Justin are a little friendly, but nothing that crosses a line, considering she wants to be with Joe.

Dustin and Tessa are lost in each other. I swear I've gotta have a talk with that girl. Dylan pulls me into his chiseled chest and doesn't let go. He kisses the top of my head, tells me how much he enjoyed tonight, and makes his way to the Mustang. Again, he plays the gentleman card.

Dustin follows him shortly, and we wave goodbye. Once they are out of sight, we sit on the front porch swing for a minute.

Every bit of adrenaline has vanished from my body. I just want to crash, but I have to keep up the act in front of our parents.

"Char, Dustin said he'd text when he knew Dylan was in for the night. That way you knew you were safe to go to Cash."

"Thanks, Tess, you're the best."

"I try. What can I say?"

"There you go with that smartassness again!"

"This is kinda off the subject, but did you see Dylan's reaction to the Joe comment?" Tessa asks.

"Yeah, it was almost as if he wanted you two together. You don't think…"

Piper interrupts me, "No, Char, don't go there! Joe is on our team. Remember?"

"I know, but I can't help but let my mind wonder."

"Well, stop that shit, okay?!"

I know I've crossed a line, but I can't help but think. I've been burned more than once, and it will not happen again.

"Sorry, Piper. So, how did I do tonight?"

"Girl! You were on it, especially when you didn't take his normal shit! I wanted to be like, 'Go Charley!' But I thought that might be a giveaway."

"Um, but Char, I will say the view we got from the porch was sickening if I do say so myself. Now, if that would have been you and Cash, I could have handled it, but Dylan's hands on you like that… ewwww!"

"You're not lying. Where's the sanitizer? I almost feel like I need a shower before I go to the club."

"Well, if you do, you better put something hot back on because Cash will be disappointed."

"Thanks, Piper, but I knew that much already. Let's go help clean up, so I can see my knight in a pair of Carhartts."

I lock my arms in each one of theirs, and we go inside and help Mama clean up. Tessa even helps and doesn't go missing.

Once the food is put away and the house is somewhat back in order, we head upstairs to my room. Mama and Dad do the same.

Once we are inside my room, I check my phone. I have one text from Dylan, and Tessa has one from Dustin.

Dylan: thanks 4 a great night, hope santa's good 2 u!

I quickly reply.

Me: Right back at ya, been helping clean up, exhausted we're going to bed, night.

Dylan: night

"He's at home, and I told him I'm exhausted and going to bed. What did Dustin say, Tessa?"

"He said they were just hanging out at home. He thinks you're good."

"Well, I'm gonna go brush him outta my mouth. Will you text Cash Money?"

"You bet! You want me to tell him to pick you up at the barn?"

"Yeah, I don't want to be out there alone. I just don't feel right."

"Make sure you take your phone in case Dustin texts me, okay? He's gonna keep tabs till you get back, so don't be gone all night if you can help it."

"I'll try... nah, I promise not to be out all night."

Within ten minutes, I'm climbing out of the window and making my way to Cash at the barn. I can hear the hum of the four-wheeler as I approach.

Before I have time to think, I'm no longer walking. I'm running as fast as my new boots will let me go.

He is waiting in the moonlight with his arms crossed and a smile spread across his face.

"Hey, Cash Money, I've been waiting on this all night."

"Not as much as I have, Char-coal. Come here," he replies as he holds me tight. "Come on. Let's get outta here."

Once we are at the club, it's obvious that he's been here waiting. The heater is on, but more importantly, he has made this horrible night special. He brought PB&J sandwiches and Choice Cherry Gold.

"Cash, I'm so full! But, I can't not eat our special meal."

"Don't feel like you have to. I just wanted a little something else up here to remind you of us."

Suddenly, it feels like my heart has been ripped out of my chest. "Cash..."

"Don't, Char-coal. I'm okay. Well... maybe...I'm handling this the best I can."

"I'm sorry."

"No, I'm sorry I had to see the back porch scene." I am completely humiliated and nauseous.

"Oh, Cash, I didn't want that to happen, but I had to make him believe."

"Shhh." He places his index finger over my lips. "No more about that. This is a night we have been waiting on."

"I love you, Cash Money, and I always will."

"I love you, too, my Char-coal. Thank God you didn't change. That dress is what has gotten me through the night."

"That's why I bought it. For you. I knew you'd love it."

"I don't care if you're wearing a trash bag, I'll love you no matter what," he says as he pulls me in for a sweet kiss that makes my leg pop.

We take a seat on the futon and share a sandwich and drink. As we fill each other in on the events of the past week, I realize that this plan might take down Dylan, but I'm losing precious moments with people that matter the most in my life.

"So, are you ready to exchange presents?" I ask.

"If you want to. You want to go first? I bet you've been dying to give it to me all night."

"You know me too well." I take the envelope from my side and pass it to him. He takes extra time opening it to torture me, and then he pulls out two rectangle pieces of paper and reads the print.

"Here's to the Good Time Tour…we're going to see FLAGALine?" I shake my head quickly. "I love it, Char-coal, but you do know this gift is one you bought for yourself, too."

"Ya got me!" I wink. He places them beside him and closes the distance between us.

"Is it okay if I take Tessa instead?" he inquires as his lips graze mine.

"You most certainly may not," I say as I close the gap and continue to show him how much he means to me.

Cash pulls away and removes a box from his jacket pocket. My heart begins to beat erratically because there is no way there is a diamond in that box. But, what if there is? I'd be the happiest girl in the world.

As if reading my mind, Cash lets me down easy. "Char-coal, it's not that, but one day it will be."

My heart sinks. I should have known because Cash would do this right. He would ask my parents for permission, make a perfect night, Dylan wouldn't be in the picture, and he would give me my happily ever after.

Taking the box, I unwrap the red chevron paper and open a small ring box. I am instantly at a loss for words. Staring at me is a chic silver circle ring. It's simple, elegant, and the meaning behind the circle is what this ring is about.

Cash takes the box from me, removes the ring, and places it onto my ring finger.

"Char-coal, you have been my beginning, and you will be my end. You complete me in every way possible, and when all of this comes full circle, just know that we are never ending, just like this circle," he tells me as he embraces the ring on my hand.

Tears build in my eyes. "Cash, I love it, but I'm so scared. What if it doesn't end the way we want it to? What if I end up alone, lonely, or never able to rid myself of Dylan? What if I lose you?"

"That won't happen, Char-coal, because I will never let you be lonely. You deserve more. You deserve happiness with a man who worships you regardless of your faults, knows your fears, and won't let anything come between you." Taking my face in his hands, he continues, "I am that man. I promise that I will never give up on you, me or us. We will make it, and this is my reminder. Just like your necklace, I'm your anchor that keeps you grounded and makes you complete. I love you, Charley Anne Rice, and I always will."

The tears begin to fall, and Cash makes it better by kissing them away. As I begin to let Cash in, forget the day and the plan I've made, and lose myself in him, my phone chirps and then Cash's does the same. I try to ignore it, but it continues to blow up. Cash and I separate and look at our phones. Panic. Sheer panic is written all over both of our faces.

Group Text:

Tessa: Dylan left house & on way here! HURRY!!!!!!!!!!!!!!!!!

My breathing begins to increase, and I feel like I'm going to hyperventilate. Cash is terrified. We hurry down the ladder and to the four-wheeler. We haul ass back to the house without our lights on.

"Cash, you might want to let me walk back instead of getting too close."

"Hell no!"

I don't argue; I hold on to him tighter as we approach the house. There aren't any lights on other than my room, no cars are out of place, and there has been no other word from Tessa.

Cash leaves the four-wheeler and helps me to the house and up to my room. Before I climb up, I turn. "I love you, Cash Money, with every ounce of my being."

"Char-coal, I love you more than life itself, but get your ass in there before shit hits the roof!"

"Okay." I kiss him quickly and hurry inside. I start to watch him walk away when Piper tells me to change and act like I've been here all night.

"Will you make sure Cash makes it back to the four-wheeler and outta here? He's gonna text when he gets back."

"Sure."

I undress in record time, wash my face, and pray that I don't smell like Cash. For once in my life, I don't want his scent on me because that could be a dead giveaway with Dylan.

As I crawl into bed, Tessa's phone chirps. Cash is home safe. No sooner has she hit the *Lock* button is there a tap at the window. I don't need to glance. I know it's Dylan. Sliding out of bed, I open the window and ask him what the hell he's doing here.

"I just had to see you again tonight, Charley. Oh, hey, Tessa and Piper." They wave, and I realize that that prepaid phone is sitting two feet from us. *Oh shit!* Quickly, I make eye contact with Piper, and she reads my mind. While I distract him with a kiss, she hides it.

Dylan laces his hands in mine and plays with the ring on my finger.

"What's this, Charley?"

"Piper gave it to me for Christmas. Do ya like it?"

He looks at both of us confused. "Yeah, it's different. Looks like something she'd buy ya. Look. I'm sorry I came by late again, but I just had the need to see your beautiful face again and bring your Christmas gift to you."

"Oh, Dylan, you shouldn't have. I didn't get you anything because this all happened so fast."

"No worries. Here ya go." He gives me a small box. "Sorry it's not wrapped. I got it late today right as they were closing."

"It's okay." I open the box to see a small, simple bracelet. It's a silver cuff with the famous *Finding Nemo* line, "Just keep swimming". He takes the bracelet and fastens it onto my wrist.

"Charley, I know things haven't been good between us, but I want you to have faith. I want you to swim, not sink. I can help you if you trust me."

I'm in complete shock. Who is this person standing in front of me?

"I'm working on it." Is all I can reply.

He kisses my cheek and then leaves. Just like that, he leaves. I stand there and watch him climb out of the window, down the roof, and to his car. I turn to Piper and

Tessa who have the same look. What the hell just happened?

Chapter 22

"What the hell was that, Charley?" Tessa asks.

"I have no clue, but I do know that is totally not like him. Do you think he knows?" I say as I make my way back to the bed.

Tessa wastes no time calling Dustin to see what else he knows. Dustin assures us that Dylan doesn't know what is going on, but he got very adamant about seeing me. He even said his entire demeanor changed.

"What do you mean 'changed'?" I ask Tessa.

"Like he couldn't get you off his mind, had to touch you, and let you know that he's changed."

"Are you fucking kidding me? He's crazy. There is no way he has changed since Study Day. That was only two weeks ago."

"Charley, we believe you, but maybe he's got a real mental problem," Piper states.

"Ya think?" I say smartly.

"Hey, let me see that ring I gave ya." Piper smiles.

I show them my ring finger, and they both stare.

"Charley, that is gorgeous. I love the circle. You know what they mean, don't you?" she says.

"Yeah, they mean forever. He told me he would never leave me no matter how this turns out, but I'm scared. What if it doesn't end like I plan? What if Cash isn't here in the end?"

"Char, don't talk like that. He's been your forever before you knew what forever meant. There are some things in life that the forces don't mess with, and y'all are one of them."

Piper gives me a hug, and we try to take our mind off things when my prepaid phone rings. Glancing at the screen, I recognize the perfect number.

"Hey, Cash Money, are you okay?"

"Me, okay? You're worried about me?"

"Well, yeah, I mean, I didn't know if he was going to you next. I'm just terrified he's gonna hurt you."

"He won't, and if so, I'm ready."

"How are you ready?"

"Don't you worry your sweet self over it. I will handle it if things get bad, but what did he want?"

"He wanted to see me and give me a Christmas gift."

"Are you fuckin' kiddin' me? We can't have one night where he tries to steal my thunder."

I make my way off the bed and open the window to climb onto the roof. Tessa tosses a blanket to me.

"Listen, Cash, it means nothing. Yes, I hate that he ruined our night, but it just means that we are one step closer to our forever. You hear me? Our forever. Please don't do anything to stoop to his level."

I don't hear any words on the phone, just slow, shallow breathing. Then, he speaks.

"Char-coal, no matter what you might think, each time I see you with him or he one-ups me, I want to beat his ass. I want to show him how much I love you and that you belong to me, not him. Tonight at the party, I went missing because I couldn't take it. Later, I had to see that display of non-affection on the back porch. I'm losing my mind, and it's only been a little over a week. If I'm not careful, I'm going to lose my sanity."

"Cash, please come get me."

"I don't think it's safe."

"But… but, I need you. You're my antidote to this hell I'm currently in."

"No, Charley, I'm not. It puts us both at a risk."

"Pleaseeeee Cash," I squall through a monsoon of tears.

"Stop, Char-coal. Stop. I can't hear you like this."

"I'm. Tryin'. To. Stop. But. I. Need. You. Now."

"I'm on my way. Char-coal, I love you, but I don't want to chance our happily ever after."

"We won't." We disconnect, and I wrap the blanket around me and wait on my Cash Money. I can see him in the distance, and he makes his way to the roof. We sit outside in the chill of the night. He holds me tight, and I know it will be okay.

"Cash, can you stay with me?"

"Um, that might be weird. Piper and Tessa are both in there."

"It's not like we didn't do this all the time growing up."

"Char-coal, as much as I want to say yes, I'm saying no. I want to keep you safe, and that doesn't. It allows more opportunity to get discovered." I pout my bottom lip. "Now, that's not fair! How about this? I'll hold you till you go to sleep, then I'll go home."

"It's not exactly what I want, but I'll take it." We stand, and I take his hand and guide him into my room. I slide into the middle of the bed, and Cash follows me, wrapping his arms around mine, and again I'm safe in Cash Money's arms.

As I wake up, I roll over and my heart plummets when I feel the side of the bed is empty. He left. I roll back over and realize that it's Christmas morning.

Piper has already gone since it's Christmas, and Tessa is on the floor sprawled out with no covers. I shake my head and then roll onto Cash's side because it makes me feel close to him.

As I'm about to doze off, Tessa jumps up. "Santa's here! Get up, Char. Let's go."

Taking the pillow, I cover my face and scream. I can't believe she's already up. She pulls the covers off the bed, and I jump to grab them, but she keeps them out of reach.

"Aight, I'm going."

I slowly roll out of bed and check my phones. Nothing. Not a word from Cash, Dylan, or anyone.

We make our way downstairs to see what Santa has brought. At almost adulthood, I still believe in Santa, because if I didn't, I wouldn't get jack. My parents always made sure we had what we needed, but more importantly, knew the reason for the holiday.

"Whatcha got, Tess?"

"Ah, ya know, clothes, money, and a new iPhone."

"Shut up!" I yell as I dig in my stocking. "Santa, please be good to me!" He is. There is a brand spanking new iPhone 5c in pink. As we finish, Mama and Dad are overlooking our excitement.

"Girls, I take it Santa was good to ya?" Dad says.

"Yup! So, when's breakfast?"

"Charley, we just got up. Give me a minute to get a cup of coffee in me, and I'll get it going," Mama says.

We all go into the kitchen to help Mama with the coffee. I take a cup for us girls. Dad won't touch the stuff.

Tessa and Mama fix theirs just alike, black. I, on the other hand, want coffee with my cream.

We sit at the table while Mama begins to prepare breakfast. The aroma of bacon, sausage, and homemade biscuits fills the kitchen. Dad is in the living room finding Christmas music on the radio. Finally, he locates one he likes, and of course, it makes me laugh. They are playing "Christmas Don't be Late" by The Chipmunks. Tessa and I look at each other and laugh. That is so Dad.

Once the biscuits are golden brown, we eat a hearty homemade breakfast and then unwrap the presents under the tree after my grandparents arrive.

Everything is exactly how it should be. My family and I at home, enjoying each other's company. I know that I belong in Grassy Pond, and I know that I will return here once I graduate from Southern. There is only one thing that will make this morning complete. Cash. My thoughts are interrupted by a knock at the door.

Chapter 23

"Merry Christmas to you, too, boys," Dad says as he stands at the door.

Tessa and I turn our attention to the front door to see Dustin and Dylan. Still in our pajamas, we get up to make our way to meet them.

"Merry Christmas, y'all two," I say as we welcome them with a hug. "Y'all wanna come in?"

"Nah, we just wanted to wish your family a Merry Christmas. We are going out of town this afternoon to Gramp's house in Charleston, so we won't be back for a few days."

"Oh… well, that sucks."

I hear Mama comment, "Charley Anne, watch your mouth."

"Yes, ma'am." I lead Dylan into the living room, and Tessa and Dustin follow. "How long are y'all gonna be gone? I mean, y'all will be back by New Year's, right?"

"Oh yeah, we should be back by Thursday." Inside my heart skips a beat because I can relax, but I need to play it down. I place my hand on his leg. "I really wish you didn't have to go."

"Me too, but Gramps is expecting his boys. It's this big deal when we go at Christmas. We have a big shootout."

"Fun! You know I'd beat ya though."

"Yes, you don't have to rub it in."

"I guess when you get back, the Kluft girls will be here. We are all gonna practice together at GPAC. You should join us."

"I think I will. Well, we better get goin'. Mom and Dad should have everything ready to go when we get back. It was good to see you again, Mr. and Mrs. Rice."

"You too, Dylan," Mama says, and Dad nods.

We walk them both to the front porch and outside.

"Thanks for stopping by, Dylan." I lean up and kiss him. "Behave while you're gone, and I'll see ya when ya get back."

As I step back, he pulls me in close again. His lips ravish mine like he's trying to make this last until he returns.

Knowing Mama and Dad are on the other side of the door, I pull away and place my hand on his chest. "Guess we better calm it down. They might be watchin," I say as I point to the window. He smiles, and it almost hurts because he looks so good.

"I'll see ya, Charley. Merry Christmas, Tessa. You ready, Dustin?"

Dustin kisses Tessa bye and walks to the Mustang while catching glimpses of her over his shoulder.

When I open the door, I see Mama and Dad getting the presents out from under the tree. Tessa and I jump in to help them.

Other than making piles of presents, there is no order to our gift opening. It's pure chaos. We don't take turns to see what everyone gets; it's just see who opens the fastest.

We pause when Dad opens his gift from us. It's a photo of *the one* and me. Tessa took the picture and made an awesome frame.

"Char, now that's what I'm talking about. Tess, you made the frame, didn't you? It's perfect. You have a talent, you know."

"Thanks, Dad. I wish I could open my own store or do something, but I just don't know how it'd go over."

"Well, I believe you would do great."

"Hey, Mama, whatcha think of those pajamas?" Tessa asks.

"They're perfect! I can always use a new pair of those. The little martini glasses are too cute."

"We thought that looked like you," I say with a smile.

We enjoy everyone's company, clean up the massive amount of wrapping paper from the floor, take our gifts to our rooms, and get ready for a day of celebrating Jesus' birth with friends and family with no threat of Dylan to interfere.

Getting ready, I decide to look a little festive. I pull on a red long-sleeved shirt, jeans, and boots. I accent my wardrobe with a pair of Christmas tree earrings that Mama gave me when I was eight. I wore them all the time until I realized it wasn't cool to wear them anymore, especially in mid- July.

I go to see if Tessa's ready and to inquire if Cash has called or texted her this morning. I knock and walk in.

"Are you not ready yet?" I ask.

"What does it look like?" she answers as she stands there half-dressed with her hair still wet from her shower. "You're as slow as a snail. It's not like Dustin's around or anything."

"Well, you look like you're trying to impress someone yourself, Charley, and those earring set it off," she says with a smart ass attitude and her hand on her hip.

"Don't be jealous. You know you have a pair, too."

"I do, don't I? Maybe I should wear them, too. It would make Mama's day." She finishes getting ready, and I borrow her phone.

Tessa: Hey $ it's me. Merry Christmas.

Cash: Merry Christmas Char-coal! I love you!

Tessa: I love you 2.

Knowing that he is about to respond to my text, I call him to hear his voice instead.

"Merry Christmas, Cash Money! Was Santa good to ya?'"

"I'm talkin' to you, so yes, he's been good to me. How about you? Did you get everything you wanted?"

"Almost. I want you here now, and I know that can't happen. But, I think this will make your Christmas.

Dylan's gone to see his gramps until Wednesday. Do you know what that means?"

"Damn right, I do! That means you and me!"

"Yup! What are y'all's plans for the day? We just finished presents, breakfast, and now are just hanging out until supper."

"That's about like us. We do have to go by Aunt Joan's for lunch, but that's it."

"So, does this mean that you'll stay with me tonight?"

"Char-coal, I didn't want to leave last night, but I was afraid that someone would catch us. Yes, I'll stay with you tonight."

"I can't wait. I guess just text Tessa or call me later. This just might be the best Christmas ever."

"No, Char-coal, this isn't the best, but it is the first of many to come. I plan on making each one better than the last. I love you, and I plan on proving that to you each and every day of my life."

"Cash, I love you so much, and I hope to do the same. Enjoy your day with your family, and I can't wait to see you tonight."

After hanging up, I text all the Kluft girls to wish them a Merry Christmas and ask them about coming to Grassy Pond for New Year's Eve. Within seconds, there are all kinds of Merry Christmas wishes, pictures, and hell yes's for New Year's. Of course, Hayden's text is priceless.

Hayden: Hell yeah! That means I can get one of those cowboys to kiss me at midnight! I'm in!

Me: Country boy, Hayden, not cowboy. Get it right ;)

Tessa and I laugh as we read the comments. The stress-free day has lightened both of our moods, and we can enjoy Christmas for what it's meant to be. Once Tessa is finally ready, we go downstairs to hang out with the family.

Grandma and Mama are sitting around the table with cups of coffee. Tessa and I fill our own cups and sit with them.

"Girls, I'm so proud of who you have become. I'm glad to say that y'all are my granddaughters."

Thanks, Grandma, but we haven't really done anything," I say.

"Yes, you have. I've watched you two grow into fine young ladies. You make me and the rest of your family proud. Keep it up."

"We'll try," Tessa says, and I feel an ache in my heart. If my grandma only knew the real me and what I was doing right now, she'd be embarrassed, heartbroken, and ready to beat Dylan's ass.

We spend the remainder of the day helping Mama and Grandma prepare for the big meal and watching holiday movies. Oh, wait! We watch *A Christmas Story* over and over.

"Tess, please turn the dang channel. I'm sick and tired of watchin' this movie. I need something other than a leg lamp and a BB gun!"

"One more time, Char. Please?" I look around the room. Our parents and grandparents have now joined us. I glance in their direction to see if their thoughts meet mine, and they do. It is so obvious.

"Um, no. Change it. Anything but this again. I think everyone in this room agrees."

"Fine." She huffs and then reluctantly gives in. We decide on the *Hallmark Channel*, and before we are twenty minutes into the movie, all the men in the room are asleep. Thank goodness they aren't sawing logs.

After the movie, we all excuse ourselves to the kitchen. Tessa and I complete the final touches on the desserts while Mama and Grandma finish the ham and sides.

"Girls, what are you going to do since the guys in your life are gone?"

I look at Tessa, and we both shrug.

"I guess I'll be at the pool most of the time, but the Kluft girls are coming to celebrate New Year's in the big city of Grassy Pond."

Mama stops mid-stir on the macaroni and cheese. "Were you planning on telling me this when they got here?"

"No, well, we just kinda finalized it this morning. We wanted to get together, and Hayden and Anna are dying to find them a cowboy."

Grandma chimes in, "Cowboy? Are they confused? There are no cowboys in Grassy Pond."

"I know. Cash even told Hayden that, but they are Yankees and don't know the difference between country and cowboy. That's why they wanna come."

"I think that's a great idea. I'd just like a little notice. Y'all going to the McCracken's farm?" Mama asks.

"Yup."

"You do know that you're gonna have to help me get this house back together for them to come. There is no way I want new guests to see it like this."

"Mama, you had a party here last night, and now it's a holiday. We'll help ya, but they aren't gonna care."

"That might be the case, but I do."

Once the food is ready, we all gather around the dining room table. You would think that the way Mama is with Thanksgiving that she would be the same way with Christmas, but she's not. Instead, she just wants us to relax, eat until we are stuffed, and enjoy each other's company.

When we finish eating, Tessa and I take care of the dishes and let the adults relax. Dad and Grandpa watch the football game. Mama and Grandma watch it with them, even though I think they could care less.

"Hey, Tessa, you got my back tonight?"

"You know it, but something just doesn't feel right to me."

"Watcha mean?"

"I just feel like this has been too easy. He is liable to surface at some point, like last night. That was crazy. Something is way off, but Dustin doesn't know anything." She stops mid-sentence. "Char, you don't think…"

"No, I don't think that Dustin is keeping anything from us. He has been nothing but helpful."

"I know I shouldn't doubt him, but I just worry that he has those bad genes."

As I let the water release from the sink, I turn to look at her. "There is no way he is like him. I've seen how he looks at you, and I know he loves you. There is absolutely no way he is like Dylan."

"Thanks, Sis. I just doubt sometimes because Dylan is his brother. It's kinda like, how do they even come from the same family?"

"I know. That's one thing I've never understood. How do wonderful parents produce children that are so far from their morals and values?"

Once we finish the dishes, we return to the living room. The sun is starting to set, and it's time to settle in for the night, or at least, make it look like I am.

"I think we are going up to my room to find another good movie."

Grandma pipes in, "How about a round of cards before you go up? Anyone wanna play?"

My grandma loves a good game of cards, and who in their right might mind would tell their grandmother no? Tessa and I look at each other, and then she goes to get a deck of cards. We all meet at the dining room table and play a few rounds of Go Fish.

After Tessa beats us all four times, we throw in the cards, swear she's a cheater, and retire to our rooms. Tessa comes to hang out with me and lets me know that Cash is on his way to get me.

I take a minute and freshen up in the bathroom before I climb out of the window and make my way to meet him at the barn. After our night got interrupted last night, I can't wait to try to finish what we started.

That's weird. He's not here yet. I wait for him on the inside of the barn. I check on the horses and almost jump out of my skin when I hear the door open.

I turn around and see Cash standing there. "Char-coal, it's just me," he says as he makes his way toward me.

I put down the feed bucket and turn to meet him. I throw my arms around him, and he lifts me off the ground and spins me in a circle.

"Merry Christmas, Char-coal," he declares as he puts me back down and kisses my lips. I don't want him to stop. I want his lips on me forever, but he pulls away. "Let's get outta here."

"Aight, a night at the club sounds good to me."

We arrive at the club, and it's almost like we are repeating last night.

When I reach the top, I gasp. "Cash! You shouldn't have." The club is lit up on the inside with Christmas lights from top to bottom. It's like a mini prom just for us.

Looking at the small table, I see a twenty ounce Choice Cherry Gold and two goblets. Cash excuses himself and places a CD into the player.

"When did you have time for this?"

"I wanted to do it last night, but it didn't work out. I made a CD of all the songs that make me think of us the other night. I wanted you to hear it with me for the first time. When those plans changed last night, I thought I was going to have to wait for who knows how long. Then, you told me he was gone, and I spent my free time today on this."

"It's like a fairytale. I love it… and you." Cash starts the CD, stands and walks toward me. Track number one is a no-brainer; it's Luke Bryan's "Crash my Party". He sings every word as he holds me in his strong and safe arms. I close my eyes and soak him in. He smells like clean sweat and the woods. His touch is rough, yet tender, and his voice is like liquid gold. Without opening my eyes, our lips meet and he tastes like wintergreen mixed with sweet cherries.

As the song ends and track two begins, I get lost in where I am, who I'm with, and what is going on outside these four walls. I need Cash Money. I want every part of him.

Trying to make sure that Cash knows what my mind is thinking, I feel him pull away.

"Cash, please don't pull away."

"Char-coal, I promised you that nothing would happen until our wedding night, and I mean that."

"But, what if that doesn't happen?" He stops and a streak of pain flashes in his eyes.

"What do you mean, Char-coal?"

"What if the plan doesn't work, and I can't escape him? What if you don't get the chance to show me?"

"Listen to me. Remove that thought from your mind because we will get our happily ever after. Don't you ever doubt that!"

"It's just that even Tessa was starting to doubt Dustin today. It made me think that I can't control everything but here and now... and right now, I want you." I trail my index finger down his chest. I can feel his breaths increase even as he tries to slow them.

Cash closes his eyes when my hands reach the top of his belt. "Char... we can't. This isn't what tonight is about."

I pause and give him a quick kiss. "Then. What. Is. This. About?" I slowly punctuate between each kiss.

Taking every ounce of control, Cash answers, "Tonight's about the start of a foundation. One that we will base the rest of our lives upon. I want you, Charley Anne, more than anything I've ever desired in my entire life. But, when we become one, I don't want any what ifs, fears, or unknown outcomes. I want you completely. That's why we can't."

Knowing that I will not win this, I pull myself close to him again as we sway our hips back and forth to the music. I close my eyes and forget about everything but Cash Money and me.

Chapter 24

I awake to the sound of the wind blowing outside the club. I smile once I take a minute to realize where I am. Last night was perfect. Our club, Cash Money, and I... alone.

Cash's arms are wrapped around me, and I want to stay in them forever, but I know I need to get back before Mama realizes I'm not home. *Shit!* I hope Dad's not out on the farm already.

I begin to move, but Cash squeezes his arms tighter. Deciding exactly how he needs to wake up, I roll toward him, trail my hands up his chest, and place my lips onto his. Once he is very much awake, I pull away from him.

"Mornin', Cash Money."

He smiles a half-grin and guides my lips back to his. Our make-out session continues, and then Cash slows the movements. He stops and stares at me.

After not being able to take it anymore, I speak.

"What?" I say sweetly, tilting my head and allowing my hair to brush his face.

"I just want to take every bit of you in and sear it in my mind, so that no matter what is going on, we are together."

"Cash, we will always be together. You're my forever, and I'm yours, right? You're not doubting, are you?"

"No, but I do have to share you with someone... someone that I want to hang out back and skin him like a deer. You are what gets me through this."

"How about we make the best days of our lives while Dylan's gone?"

"Sounds like a perfect plan to me. Where do you want to start?"

"Well, I have an idea," Cash says as he pulls me closer to him.

"I think I like your idea."

Cash's lips ignite mine, and I do have to say that I'm starting to understand the importance of us waiting because there is so much more that can happen besides that.

Seeing the sun begin to get higher in the sky, I know I have to leave Cash, but knowing with the absence of Dylan I don't have to put him in a bad position makes the day brighter.

"Hey, Cash, I need to get back. Dad will be at the barn soon, if he isn't already."

"I know." He kisses me briefly, and we make our way out of the club.

"Look. I'm going to try to get you as close to the house as possible, but help me look out."

"Maybe I should call Tessa?"

"Great idea, Char-coal. Sometimes I miss the obvious."

Grabbing Cash's phone, I call Tessa. Dad is in the house, so we know we have a few minutes. Jumping on the four-wheeler, we make our way to the barn. Cash kisses me quickly, and I hurry to the house and into my window where Tessa is standing to help me back in.

Turning around, I see Cash watching. I blow him a kiss, he catches it, and pulls it to his heart. My heart just melted.

Rushing to help Dad with the morning chores, I change clothes and hurry downstairs to go to the barn.

"Hey, Charley! Glad to see you this morning," Dad says from the living room.

"I was just about to go to the barn to help ya. You're a little later than normal, aren't ya?"

"Yeah, this old man needed a few extra minutes. My back is all stove up."

"You really need to take it easy. I'll be glad to help while I'm home."

"I know, but you also have to train and your friends are coming. It's just all those years of football catchin' up with me."

"Well, ol' man, I might be able to help ya out."

Dad and I make our way to the barn. I take the bale of hay to the horses, slop the hogs, and check on the goats while he collects the eggs from the chickens. We take care of everything in record time. Dad informs me that he needs to do a little maintenance to the tractor shed.

"You want me to help?"

Dad gives me a look that expresses the need for me to drop the subject.

"Char, I might have been a little slow moving this mornin', but I ain't going to the old folks home just yet."

"Aight, I get it, Dad. I'll see you after practice."

I leave Dad while he gathers his tools to work and go back to the house. While Mama is putting the finishing touches on breakfast, I hurry upstairs and grab my bag. I walk through the kitchen, talk to her a minute, grab two pieces of bacon, a Choice Cherry Gold and make my way to GPAC.

The sets aren't too bad today. Enjoying the fact that Dylan won't be there, I soak in the environment. Since this is like my second home, I take a few extra minutes to enjoy it without any games being played.

As I get out of the pool, Coach motions for me to come toward him.

"What's up, Coach?"

"Just checking to see how your holiday has been. I wanted to make sure everything was okay... with you and Dylan."

That catches me off guard. "Everything's fine. Why do you ask?"

"Charley, you are one of the top swimmers to ever come through GPAC. You are so much stronger than Dylan, but don't tell him I said that. You could have easily gone Division One, but you didn't. Just don't let him hold you back. You have bigger and better things in your future."

"Thanks, Coach. Coming back to the pool is the best decision I've ever made. If the girls at Southern hadn't pushed me, I wouldn't be here now."

"I'm glad you have a strong foundation, and I think you might have some awesome news once you get back."

Coach has my curiosity piqued. I wonder what he knows.

Coach dismisses me, and I hurry to get back home. I have a lot to do before the Kluft girls arrive, and I know that Mama isn't gonna let me out of her sight until that house is put back to her standards.

On my way to the house, my phone rings, glancing at the screen I cringe... Dylan. Putting on my game face, I answer with the giddiness of a teenager at a Justin Bieber concert.

"Hey!"

"Well, hey, Charley! You sound like you're having a great morning without me." *Crap! That wasn't what I expected.* "Was the pool that much better without me?" he questions.

"Uh...It was nice to have it all to myself, but Coach said something to me that has me excited."

"Really? What?"

"I'm not sure. He just said that I have some news waiting when I get back to Southern."

"I'm sure it will be well worth the wait. So, what do you have planned today?"

"Mama has my day planned, but I was able to help Dad on the farm before practice. Let's just say that since the Kluft girls are coming, Mama wants the house spotless. Other than that, I'm sure Piper, Tessa, and I will hang out. Maybe I can talk Piper into helping me clean."

"Yeah, good luck with that! That's about like Tessa helping out."

That comment makes me laugh because it is so true.

"I guess you're right, but hey, it was a thought."

"Well, we are going to visit more family today. Then, all the cousins are going to some bar later. They said it's like Turtle's, but with a dance floor. It should be interesting."

In a pouting voice, I reply. "Just make sure you miss me. I sure could use a dance or two with you."

"Oh, no one will take your place, and I agree a night of dancing is what we need. Too bad we didn't get to at Whiskey River."

"I know… there will be another time, I'm sure."

"You can bet on it." The comment sends chills up my spine, and I'm glad I'm now on my long driveway.

"Well, I'm home. Guess I better get this cleaning over and done with."

"Good luck, Charley. I'll call you before we go out tonight. Oh, and I miss you."

"Sounds good. I miss you, too."

We disconnect, and I enter the house. I can see that Mama has already gotten the boxes down to put away the Christmas decorations. Tessa is cleaning the kitchen. *Impressive.*

"Want some help, Tess?"

She tosses me the drying towel, and we finish in no time. Within seconds of finishing the dishes and wiping the counter, Mama is waiting to get started on removing the ornaments from the tree.

"Girls, y'all get the ornaments off while I gather the other whatnots around the house."

"Yes, ma'am," we both say.

Tessa turns on *CMT*, and we sing and dance as we undress the tree. We laugh, act silly like we are five years old, and enjoy our time together. One other constant in my life is Tessa. She's the one that understands me and what I'm going through. She's also the one who has covered for me in ways that I didn't know were possible. Even though I give her a lot of crap about always being gone when work is to be done, she's never missing when I need her most.

"Hey, Tessa… thanks."

"For what?"

"For not leaving when I needed you most," I say as I bump into her shoulder.

"Char, you know I'm always here. I'd never run when you need me to stand beside you. You're my sister, and I will never break that promise to you... never."

Our loving moment is interrupted by Mama. "Great! Now let's get this tree to the burn pile and these boxes to the loft in the barn."

After helping Mama remove the decorations from the house, we then begin the task of cleaning. Starting with downstairs, Tessa dusts while I clean the bathrooms, and Mama vacuums.

Once we finish our tasks, Tessa and I head to our rooms to clean our disaster areas. Surprisingly, it doesn't take as long as I had imagined, but I'm exhausted once we are done. I'm not sure if it's from cleaning or everything else going on in my life—my late night with Cash, practice, or working on the farm. Regardless, I'm ready to sit back and relax for a little while.

A week without Dylan has been exactly what I needed. I spent it with Piper, Tessa, and Cash when no one was watching.

"Charley, I need you to help me finish getting the house ready for the Kluft girls." I snicker at Mama as she refers to them as the Kluft girls.

"What's so funny?"

"Nothing." She places her hands on her hips. "Aight, it's just funny to hear you refer to them as 'the Kluft girls'. It's like you're one of us, too."

"I don't think I want to go back to college, but you can make me y'all's honorary mama. What do you think?"

"I think that sounds great. Georgia said she will be here by three with Caroline and Sarah not far behind. Tori is picking up Hayden and Anna from the airport and then coming this way. I can't wait to show them around here. They always give me crap about being so southern."

"They do it because they love ya. That I know, but quit talking and get that room cleaned up."

I hurry to my room and pick it up one last time. Tessa has even stayed around to help. Dad comes inside and needs some help with the horses, so I volunteer to go.

"Char, I can't wait to meet all the girls. You think they'd want to help on the farm tomorrow?"

"Highly unlikely, but we should act like we're gonna make 'em. Hayden and Anna's faces I'm sure will be priceless."

"I'm in. I think I'll ask them to gather eggs in the morning before you go to practice."

"Sounds good to me." The thought of those chickens pecking at Anna and Hayden's hands is too funny, but the thought of them freaking out about it is even better.

I finish helping Dad, and we head back to the house. I shower and get ready for Georgia to arrive. It's amazing how these girls have changed my life. I don't know what I'd do without them.

As three o'clock approaches, I get antsy waiting on everyone, and by the time it is three o'clock, I'm pacing the floor.

"Girl, sit down before you wear the floor out," Tessa says.

I finally sit down and wait. I keep glancing at my phone, checking the time. All of a sudden, I hear the most girl-like horn honking… it's Georgia. I jump up and sprint to the front door, fling it open, and hurry to meet her.

She jumps out of the car and squeals with excitement as we greet each other.

"Ohmygosh, Char. I love this place! It totally fits you. Oh, but you gotta get out the way. I gotta pee like a damn race horse."

"Come on." We make our way into the house, and I show Georgia where the bathroom is and take her stuff to my room. Then I hear Mama yelling that there is another car coming up the driveway. I glance out my window to see Caroline and Sarah; they must have followed each other.

"Hey, Georgia! Sarah and Caroline are here. Just meet me downstairs, okay?"

"Okay!" she yells through the bathroom door.

As I hurry to get to the front door, Mama is greeting them with open arms and freshly made chocolate chip cookies just out of the oven.

"Hey, y'all! Did y'all find it okay?" I ask.

"Yeah, except for those stoplights. You weren't kidding. That's the worst part of the entire ride," Caroline says.

"Now, you know what I'm talking about. Sarah, have you heard from Hayden?"

"Their flights were leaving on time, and they should arrive around five. So, I figure they will be here around six thirty or so."

"Awesome! Let's get y'all's stuff upstairs, and then we can hang out or go to town till they get here."

"As long as I don't have to go through those lights again, I'm game," Caroline states with sarcasm.

We decide to just hang around the farm until they get here. Mama has prepared a huge country style meal to welcome everyone, and she wants us out of the house while she finishes.

We walk to the barn, and I take them on a tour of the farm on the Gator. We start at the barn, and I introduce them to Dad, and then we make our way to the chickens, pigs, and the goats near the pond.

"Is that the world-famous club?" Caroline asks.

"Yes, it is. Y'all wanna go check it out?"

"Sure," they say in unison. We roll beside the pond and up to the club. We get out of the Gator and start up the ladder one at a time.

Halfway up, Caroline puts in her two cents, "So, Cash isn't gonna get mad that we are in y'all's sacred spot, is he?"

We all about fall off the ladder when we hear a deep, hearty, sexy voice answer, "No, I don't think he will care."

I don't need to look. I know the voice, but I do, however, want to jump from the top of the ladder into those arms below.

"Cash, catch me!" I turn and jump. Right on cue, his arms cup my body perfectly and give just enough.

"Char-coal, what would you have done if I hadn't been paying attention?"

"I guess both of our asses would have been on the ground, huh?"

He shakes his head and captures my lips. The girls have made their way up to the top of the club, and I can hear Tessa filling them in on what has been going on, and that every time Cash and I are alone we can't keep our hands off each other.

Cash puts me down and smacks me on the ass as I climb up the ladder once again. He follows me up and helps me climb in.

Once he's inside, the girls let in on me. "What the hell are you thinking, Charley? Dylan is fuckin' crazy, and you're pretending to date him! He could kill you or something. You know he's not stable."

"Chill out, Caroline. I've got this. I promise. So far, things are going just like they should. We've only had one close call, and it worked out okay. What do y'all think?" I say, trying to change the conversation.

"Nice try, Charley. We love it, and we will finish this conversation later. How long have y'all been coming here?" Sarah asks.

"As long as I can remember. I mean, it wasn't this hooked up to start with, but slowly we made it our Redneck Riviera, our own little getaway. We just got the lights, heater, and mini fridge not too long ago. Right, Cash?"

"Yeah, we are slowly moving up in this world. We might have running water and indoor plumbing before it's all over."

Caroline and Sarah look at me to gauge my reaction. "He's not kidding. We spend many a night out here, and I'd love to have a toilet! You never know what might bite your ass when you squat by a tree."

"Oh my gosh! I so wish that Hayden and Anna would have heard this conversation."

Caroline and Sarah take a few minutes to explore the club, and it doesn't take them long to see Cash's new artwork on the base of the window. Their faces light up just like mine did. Once they are ready to go, we head back.

Cash follows us down, and as I'm walking to the Gator, he grabs my hand and spins me around into him. He runs his hands through my hair and places those warm, delicate lips on mine. "I love you, Char-coal. Enjoy this time with your friends, and I'll see you New Year's Eve." He kisses me deep into my soul and backs away. He takes off on his four-wheeler and continues to look over his shoulder as he drives back to his farm.

"Hot damn, Charley! Y'all might as well have gotten naked right here in front of us!" Caroline exclaims.

"Whatever. It was not like that."

"Yes, it was, Sis. Do you want me to give a play-by-play? You know I can."

"That's all right. Please don't."

We all laugh and make our way back to the house.

As we arrive back, I can see headlights coming down the gravel drive. It's an Explorer. Here they come.

We don't bother taking back the Gator. We just drive straight to the house and meet Tori, Anna, and Hayden.

Hayden is the first one out. "Holy shit, Char, this place is freakin' huge! I think I've died and ended up on that plantation in that movie. What was it called?" We all look at each other. "You guys know what I'm talking about. Ya know, she falls on the ground and eats dirt or something."

We all look around and die laughing at Hayden. Tessa steps in, "You mean *Gone with the Wind?*"

"Yeah, that would be it! She did eat dirt, didn't she?"

"Um, no, that would have been like a turnip or something. Not dirt. What the hell? Do you think we rednecks eat dirt, and that's what makes us red?" Tessa smarts back.

"Simmer down, girl," I tell her. "Hayden, Tori and Anna, this is Tessa, my sister. She is my polar opposite."

"Hey, now, we might be polar opposites, but I know you about better than anyone."

I put my arm around her. "I know."

We make our way into the house, and I introduce everyone to my parents. I take their bags upstairs, and we all get ready for supper.

"Mama Rice, this is fabulous! What is this called?" Anna asks.

"It's country-style steak. Do you like it?" Everyone nods. "It's not steak though." Hayden and Anna stop mid-chew and stare at her. "No worries, girls. I'm just kidding... well, maybe." They both swallow their bite and then reluctantly take another one. Funny how people are fine until they know it's not cow.

"So, what is it?" Tori asks the question they all want to know.

"Deer."

"Bambi! I'm eating Bambi? Oh gosh, I'm going to hell," Hayden exaggerates.

"Hayden, you are not. Now, eat up or nothing else for the remainder of your visit," Mama says with determination.

"It is good though. I just never thought I'd eat Bambi," she replies.

Tessa nudges me and says, "Heck, it could be opossum," just loud enough for Hayden to hear. In one swift motion, she spits out her food across the table and straight at Georgia. The entire table erupts in laughter.

"I can already see this is going to be an interesting week," Mama says as she gets a rag to clean up the mess.

We finish the meal with no more accidents. Once we finish, we decide to take a ride into town.

As soon as we are in the Explorer, twenty million questions start about Cash, Dylan, me, and anything else they can come up with. I fill them in on everything, and anything I choose to leave out, Tessa fills in. Sometimes we have a love-hate relationship.

We cruise through town while I point out all the major establishments in Grassy Pond. We drive by the Burger Shak, Dixon High, GPAC, and even make our way to Turtle's Pool Hall.

"Hey, why aren't we stopping?" Hayden questions.

"Y'all wanna go to Turtle's tonight?" I ask.

"Hell yes! I need a cowboy now!" We all shake our head at Hayden. "Sorry, I mean country boy. I need my own Cash Money!"

"There is no other Cash Money, but there are some guys in the running for second and third." I wink.

Tori turns around the Explorer, and we pull into the parking lot. There are only three trucks parked.

"Now, it's a Wednesday night, so don't expect much." We all get out and go in. Sammy is working as usual. He twists off the cap of a Choice Cherry Gold and hands it to me.

Everyone else walks up to the counter. Anna bats her eyelashes, flashes her pearly whites, and asks for a Bud Light. She skids to a halt when Sammy asks for her ID. "Ah, hell, never mind then," she says as he laughs.

"Sammy, these are the Kluft girls from Southern. I'm showing them around Grassy Pond, and they insisted on coming in tonight. You think anyone will be here tonight?"

"Well, if you are referring to trouble number one and trouble number two, I heard they are out of town, but a set of three are in the corner." The triplets are the set of three. I look over and wave. Seeing them makes me think about Piper. I haven't heard from her all day. Where the hell is she? I pull out my new phone and text her. I get a quick reply.

> *Piper: Sorry been busy. I got a surprise I'll meet y'all there.*

> *Me: k, u might want to bring extra beer n ur purse.*

Once everyone has a non-alcoholic beverage, we make our way over to the triplets.

"Hey, y'all, these are my friends from Southern. That's Tori, Anna, Hayden, Sarah, Caroline, and Georgia," I say as I point to each girl.

The boys stand and introduce themselves. I can instantly tell that Hayden and Anna are eyeing Jack and Jordan. It didn't take them long. We sit with them and play a few rounds of pool. Anna and Hayden are putting it on thick with those two, and it is definitely working. I can already see they have their dates for New Year's in the works. Georgia and Justin have hit it off, and I wonder how awkward it will be when Piper gets here.

Tori, Tessa, Caroline, and I just sit back and watch. Who would have thought that my friends would have their eyes set on country boys in less than twenty-four hours in

Grassy Pond? As I think that, I notice Tori walking up to the bar. Oh shit. I know who she's eyeing. Sammy. This is going to be good.

She takes a seat at the bar and turns on the sexiness. I see Sammy glance my way and shake his head. I mouth to him, "She's legal." He winks and plays right along with her. Trying not to stare, I focus back on everyone at the table, and then I hear the door open. I look over, and it's Piper. She is decked out to the nines, and someone is coming in behind her. I do a double take. I jump up from my seat and run to them, knocking over a few chairs in my haste.

"Jackalope Joe! What are you doing here?" I pause and turn to Piper. "Hey, Piper." Then, I return my glance to Joe. "Now, what are you doing, Joe?"

"Nice to see you, too," Piper says.

"See. There's this girl I really like, and well, when she offered for me to come to some kick ass country hoe down for New Year's, I just couldn't resist."

"Oh, I see. Come on. Let's go hustle a few of them, Piper. Whatcha think?"

"Oh, I'm in. Shit! Is that Justin?"

Joe looks at her with question in his eyes. "Yeah, but no worries. He and Georgia have hit it off."

"Oh," she says with a little hurt in her voice. I can tell that Joe wants to ask, but he doesn't.

I introduce him to everyone. Piper and I do exactly what we said we would do. We hustle the Kluft girls, and Joe stands there in amazement.

As we wrap up our third game, the crowd is beginning to grow at Turtle's. Luckily, Trent and his crew are absent. I'm getting tired and know we have to go to the pool tomorrow. I try to get the girls to head out, but they are a few sheets to the wind, thanks to Piper's purse and car.

Just when I think I'm ready to go home, the door opens and my fine ass country boy struts his way in. Cash is in his worn-out Carhartts and a long-sleeved thermal. It's nothing extravagant, but it fits him and I can see the outline of his six pack through his shirt. Oh, if I were only allowed to go up to him and run my hands up and down his abs in public, but I'm not.

Cash's eyes meet mine, and he must have read my mind because he flashes a quick smile before going to grab a pool stick and joining in with a table of guys next to us. The fact that he is next to me and I'm not allowed to show what I am feeling is driving me crazy. I swear if he touched me I might explode.

The Kluft girls waste no time making a move on Cash. He goes along with their charade. The jukebox is playing all the local favorites, and when "Pour Some Sugar on Me" starts to play, the Kluft girls go wild. I join in on the fun. We take our pool sticks and dance seductively. All the guys in the pool hall gawk like they have never seen a group of girls shake it like that. We play it up and know exactly what we are doing. When the song ends, we go back to our game like nothing just happened, but something did. We made our presence known, and I know for damn sure, that Dylan has already found out. That's one downfall or perk of technology.

We finish the game and then decide to head back to the farm. Practice is going to come early. Just as I'm about to open the car door, I hear someone call my name. I stop and turn. Cash. I wave to him and get into the car. I can't stop, because if I do, then I'm going to show the world where my heart belongs.

As we drive away, I look back, and he looks lost. I wipe away the single tears that begin to stream down my face faster and faster.

Tessa places her arm around me and pulls me close as I let the tears fall. At this moment, I realize that I'm losing my forever by tempting my past. This has got to come to an end, and it has to happen before I start second semester.

When we pull onto the gravel, I wipe my eyes, take a deep breath, and pull it together before we go inside.

Of course, there is no escaping the inevitable. Mama is waiting up.

"Charley Anne, are you okay?" she lovingly questions. I try to answer, but I'm unable. My nodding yes is overtaken by tears. Mama walks to me and comforts me with her arms. "Girls, what is going on? I think it's time someone did some talkin'."

"No, Mama, it's Cash. He won't let me go."

Mama waits a few minutes as I cry on her shoulder before she answers. "Sweet girl, maybe that's because he's not meant to let go. Listen to your heart and not your head." Pulling myself away, I wipe my tears on my sleeve and quickly go upstairs with the Kluft girls right behind me.

Once the door is shut, Georgia takes control. "Aight, girls. It's time to put this plan into high gear, take down his ass, and get Char her happily ever after. So, here's the deal. We go to practice and fall at Dylan's feet. I have a feeling he will be there when we get there, but I could be wrong. Char, don't you think he'll be there?"

"I'm sure of it."

"Great. Once we make him think we are all about him, we are going to enjoy our day. Then, at the party tonight, we are taking him down."

This isn't how the plan is supposed to happen. I'm the one to take him down. This is my game. I started it, and I plan to finish it. Pulling myself from my own pity, I tell them how this is really gonna go.

"No, Georgia, that's not how it's gonna go." She looks at me like she can't believe I'm challenging her plan. To think, most people believe they can run over her, and she will take it. Actually, she's a little ball of fire, and I'd hate to be the one that she explodes on.

"Here me out. The first part is genius. Everyone needs to swoon over him. He needs to believe that y'all are all about hot, tatted, swimmer god Dylan Sloan, but when we go to the party, this is where the story changes." All of them look like they are on pins and needles listening to what I'm about to say.

"The party is in the middle of nowhere at the McCracken's farm. Since y'all have already made love connections, it's gonna make this even easier than I had thought because it won't look like I have to babysit any of you. No offense. If he's heard of our dancing at Turtle's, he's gonna expect a show of some kind tomorrow. Now, do I give it to him or not? My thought is…let's replay tonight, but turn it up a notch. I'm going to pull him to his breaking point and then back away. More than likely he won't be able to handle it, and when I tell him no, everyone around us will see it."

Georgia begins to grin, and I can see the wheels turning. "But, how are we going to blackmail him? We need some type of evidence."

"See. I have already got that covered. That's where y'all come in. You know I said technology is a love or hate relationship? Well, we are going to love it that night. I need for one of y'all or maybe two of ya to catch it on video, and then send that shit out all over the internet. His ass will be grass along with his swimming career."

"Char, that sounds perfect, but it's not gonna be that easy, ya know?" Hayden says. I don't think I have ever seen her this serious.

"Watcha mean? I know we can't all sit around and wait with a camera, but y'all are gonna know."

I start to talk more when Tessa cuts me off, "Um, they're back." Fear and anxiety overtake me once again, but instead of crying, I'm angry. I know he's going to pay me a visit tonight. I just know it.

Chapter 25

At some point in the night, we all crash. I feel like I've been hit by an eighteen wheeler, but there's no sight of Dylan and no word from Cash. I hope Cash understands why I did what I did.

We don't bother getting ready for bed; we just crash wherever we fall.

I'm awakened to the sound of beating on the window. My heart races as I walk over, but there is nothing there. Instead, I see woodpecker tapping into the power line. I've got to chill out or Dylan is gonna know something is up.

I slide back into bed, even though I realize I have to go to the pool in an hour. I toss and turn multiple times before deciding to just screw it and get up. I know Dad is up, and I can at least help on the farm before I go to practice.

I slide on my old jeans, flannel shirt, boots and camo ball cap. Dad is getting all the feed ready for the animals when I walk into the barn.

"Morning, sunshine! What brings you out here? I know y'all had a long night last night. Your mama said you were pretty upset when you got in." With that statement, a rush of emotions hits me again.

"Dad, I just can't win. Cash won't let me go, and I want to be me."

"I know that, but just know that I've only seen one other guy head over heels that much in my lifetime." I give him a questioning look. "Charley, I was Cash. The moment I realized your mama was the one for me, I knew there was no letting go. Cash isn't going to let you go, and

I know that deep down you love him, too. I'm not exactly sure what you're trying to prove by seeing Dylan again, but he's not the one for you."

I'm completely stunned by the words from Dad. He has rocked me to my core, and he knows the truth. Will he continue to play along, or is he going to start fighting for Cash and me? He goes back to fixing the buckets of feed, and I grab a basket to retrieve the eggs from the chicken house.

I finish getting the eggs and take the Gator to slop the hogs when I realize that time is getting away from me. Undoubtedly, the farm is great therapy. Hurrying back to the house, I put on my game face.

When I open the door, all the girls are downstairs eating breakfast. "Well, there you are, sweet girl. I see you had a little farm therapy this morning."

"I guess you could say that." I fix a plate and eat hastily before grabbing my swim bag. Even though Caroline, Hayden, and Anna don't need to go to GPAC, they do anyway.

Once we are in the Explorer, I give Tori directions to GPAC. She quickly stops me and tells me that she's got this.

As we approach the pool, our assumptions are confirmed when I see Dylan's Mustang in the parking lot.

"Char, you can do this. We can do this," Georgia confirms. "This is gonna be a test for all of us."

Once we are inside, I introduce them to Coach Stephens and show them around. We get the workout list and waste no time getting started on the warm-up. Dylan is working hard through a set and doesn't seem to notice us or either he's trying to show off.

We have a great practice and are balls of energy the entire time. Dylan finally notices us and pays us a visit. Tori and Sarah are the perfect fangirls, and he eats it up. What an asshole! We finish our set, and Dylan watches from the stands with the non-swimming Kluft girls. He's turning up the charm, and they are taking him for a ride. So far this plan is going like it should.

After our cool down, Dylan meets me at the end of the lane and helps me out. As soon as I'm firmly on dry land, he scoops me in for a very public display of affection.

"Dylan, stop! There are little kids in here!"

"Come on, Charley. I haven't seen you in days. I'm just glad to see you, and I can't wait for tonight."

"And why is that?" I ask as I walk with the rest of the girls to the stands.

"Let's just say I want to see that booty shaking in action. From what I heard, y'all put a hurting on some poor old boys, and I missed it. You know that ass is mine, don't ya?"

"What? You think you got papers on it or somethin'?" I smart off.

"I'd like to think so." Dylan gives me a light kiss and heads to the locker room. We follow behind and hurry to get ready. We don't want to keep the other girls waiting.

As we walk out of the locker room, I notice that Dylan is obviously soaking up this attention. He is such a fool. Hayden is being Hayden, and while she looks like she is all about him, she's actually making him look stupid in the process. We all shake our heads.

Tori looks at me. "I wonder what line she used on him."

"Oh, I can promise it had to do with a little Speedo. Whatcha think?"

"Most definitely," she replies.

We approach them, and the conversation shifts, almost like you walked in on someone talking about you.

"Did we interrupt something?" I ask.

Dylan stands and positions himself beside me while he wraps his arms around my waist. "Nope, we were just talking about tonight. I heard they are having BBQ, too. So, Dustin and I will meet y'all there?" He forms the last part as a question.

"You mean, you aren't pickin' me up?" I pout.

"I thought that might be kinda rude," he says as he motions to the girls. "Don't ya think?"

"I agree. Well, let's get outta here." We walk to Tori's Explorer. Dylan laces his fingers in mine and walks with me. He gives me a quick kiss before turning to walk to the Mustang. He glances back at me, and I wave, get inside, and close the door.

"Quick, someone give me some hand sanitizer!" They all look at me funny. "I'm serious! I've got to get these creepy germs off me now!" Caroline rummages through her purse and reveals a bottle. "Thank you! Now, I just need some mouthwash. Yuck!"

"Please tell me that you haven't been doing this each time?" Tori questions.

"Well… um… maybe."

"Yeah, we have got to make this end tonight."

We relax once we are back at home, and Mama makes us fried bologna sandwiches for lunch. Hayden is in awe.

"Y'all really do fry everything down here."

"Hayden, you need to come to the county fair. Everything is fried there."

"Like what?"

"Oreos, funnel cakes, snickers, ice cream. I really think the list is endless."

"You're kidding, right?" All the Kluft girls from south of the Mason Dixon shake our heads no.

As time approaches for the party, we take turns getting ready. Hayden and Anna have asked a million questions about what to expect about a field party. I realize it's easy to just listen about it. I crank up Brad Paisley's "Outstanding in our Field". When the song ends, they look lost.

"Y'all all right?"

"Is that how it's really gonna be? I mean, a tire for a cooler?" I shake my head yes. Hayden seems to have a light-bulb moment and then is good to go. "I'm down."

As I finish putting on the final touches of my makeup, I hear Mama calling. Piper and Joe are here. I yell for her to send them up.

"Hey, hot bitches!" Piper says as she enters.

"I think you've got that wrong, Piper. You look like you're about to go out in the city," Caroline counters.

"I also try to look my best, even when we are out in the middle of nowhere. Plus, I have one fine man beside me that I have got to look fabulous for. Isn't that right, Joe?"

His face turns red. I don't think I've ever seen that before. "Piper, you know you don't have to impress me. You're perfect just the way you are." He pulls her in and gives her a quick kiss on the side of her forehead. We all say, "Awe."

Once downstairs, I ask Dad for the keys to the Chevy. There's no way we are going to make it without four-wheel drive. Tori chimes in and says that she's got this. I look at Dad and shrug my shoulders.

We give Piper and Joe the rundown of tonight's events. They are game, and we make our way to the McCracken's farm.

Once I know that we are safe from other ears, I ask if anyone has talked to Cash. Tessa has, and he's ready.

When we pull up to the field, Tori stops the Explorer and turns the wheel locks. We all hop out, grab the beer, and make our way to the field. I have to say that I am impressed she's from the South and just made me a little bit prouder.

"So, where will we know where to go?" Anna asks.

I don't answer; I point. There is an enormous orange flame to our right.

"Holy shit!" she says.

As we approach, I see Cash talking to the triplets. We smile and move on. I take a couple of minutes and introduce the girls to several people.

While talking to Sally and a few of Tessa's friends, I feel someone's arms wrap around my waist and whisper into my ear. "You look great, Charley."

I turn, wrap my arms around him and smile. "Thanks."

The night goes on just as I expected with great music, food, drinks, and dancing. As if someone knew what we were waiting on, "Pour Some Sugar on Me" comes through the speakers. I look at the Kluft girls, and we know exactly what we have to do. In fact, we dance even more seductively than we did when we were at Turtle's.

Halfway through the song, we are no longer dancing alone. The entire crowd is shaking it, and I can feel Dylan pressed firmly against my backside. I know that the beginning of the end is about to happen. I start to panic inside. I search the crowd for Cash, but he is nowhere to be found. Then, I see him dancing with Sally. I pause momentarily.

Dylan notices me. "You know he'll never have you, right? You're mine."

"I only want to be yours, Dylan," I say as I turn to face him, kissing him slowly and seductively.

"Good." We finish dancing to the song, and then he pulls me from around the fire. I know that this is it. My heartbeat increases when I realize that I can't signal anyone; I sure hope they are paying attention and not lost in lust with anyone.

I take him by the hand and follow him to the edge of the light, and we sit on a stump. Turning to look at me, he says, "Char, you're gorgeous. You know that, don't you?" he asks as he brushes my hair behind my ear.

Biting my lip, I look into the eyes of the devil in human form. I know that is his weakness. "Don't do that, if you know what's good for ya," he says jokingly. I do it again, and he wastes no time. His lips capture mine.

I close my eyes and push away all thoughts of who is around me, the game I'm playing, and I kiss Dylan like my life depends on it, because it does.

It doesn't take Dylan long to try to turn up the heat a notch. He starts with the hem of my shirt. He toys with it a little before moving his hand underneath. I flinch at his touch, and he tells me it's okay before pushing further. I kiss him deeper, move my hands across his body, straddle him, and act as if I'm up for a Golden Globe.

Just as expected, Dylan begins to try more. The difference between tonight and the last time is that we are both in control. Neither of us has been drinking, I haven't been drugged, and yet, this monstrous side of him is rearing his ugly head again.

I pull away as he touches my breast. He stops and looks at me with those same hungry eyes he had before.

"I think we need to slow down," I whisper.

"Why? You know you want to."

"I don't think I do."

"Okay." *Okay? What the hell?* He stops for a minute, but then kisses my neck. I know that he's not going to completely stop; he's just trying to butter me up.

I let him attempt a little more during round two. I keep my eyes closed because I don't want to see who is watching, and if Cash is, it will break my heart.

Just as I expected, when he feels that he has me, he makes another bold move. This time he tries to slide his hand down my pants. I stop him. I can see that he is getting pissed off. "Not here," I whisper into his ear.

Looking like he just won the lottery, he stands and adjusts himself. We walk toward a place a little more secluded called Make-out Manor. It's a little shed on the farm. My brain goes into overdrive. What if no one follows us? When we enter the shed, Dylan uses his phone to guide me to a spot to sit. I don't hear anyone else. *Shit!* He wastes no time trying to explore my body. I give him a little leeway, but as soon as he crosses the elastic band of my panties, I start pushing him off me.

"Stop, Dylan. I need a minute. I'm not sure I want to do this."

"Come on, Char. Don't tell me you led me in here just to mess around."

"No, I thought I was, but I'm not. I want to be that girl for you, Dylan. I want to give you all of me, but I just don't know if I can."

He stops and seems to contemplate his next move. He takes a deep breath and kisses me forcefully. I try to move to offset his weight on me, but it's no use.

Dylan's movements, touches, and kisses get heavier with each moment. I push, beg, and plead with him to stop, but he continues to kiss me. "Stop! Please!" First, it's a whisper. He pushes forward. The next time my volume increases and becomes more confident and firm.

I quickly realize that he's not going to stop, and there is no one here to save me but myself. Ideas begin to race around in my mind. How am I going to get out of this? I've done it again. Maybe I can push him off me? I use all my strength, but it doesn't work. Feeling that I'm defeated again, I allow tears to trail quietly down my face as Dylan begins to try to take complete advantage of me...again. Then, as if I turned on a light, it occurs to me that this is my game, and I'm coming out on top this time.

I relax and act as if I'm giving in to his request. Closing my eyes, I focus on making Dylan feel like I belong to him. I caress his tatted and broad swimming arms, run my hands through his hair, and get lost in a kiss that will end this charade, all the while trying to keep this from crossing the line. I push things further by moving my hands down his body, yet my lips never leave his. A loud moan escapes his mouth, and I know he starts to think that I'm going all the way as I find his belt. Catching him off guard, I playfully bite his lip, causing another moan to release. Then, as he is losing himself in me, I bite the hell out of his lip. He's in complete shock. I take his moment of weakness to move from underneath him. I stand and try to find a way out in the dark.

I can see the light of the fire barely underneath the crack in the door. Hurrying across the room, I grab the handle of the door. As I pull it open, he grabs my arm. Trying not to fall back into his trap again, I yank my arm with every ounce of my being from his grasp while screaming.

"Somebody help me! PLEEEAASSSSSEEEE!" I expel from my lungs. No one. Not a soul sees us. My adrenaline kicks into high gear. I put the Ariats in the wind and haul ass to the fire.

As the roar of the fire comes into view, so do all the people. They are oblivious to what has just occurred. They continue to sing, drink, and party as I run as fast as I can. The more people I'm around, the safer I am. I see Piper and Joe sitting on a log. A look of horror flashes when she sees me, and her eyes speak volumes. I know that he is coming…that he is coming for me… it's time to face the devil with everyone watching. Knowing that I don't want to turn around and face him, I center my feelings to my core, and I do it anyway.

Dylan is within a few feet of me. He has a mix of emotions on his face that include shock, pain, and confidence, but the obvious one is rage.

"Stay away from me," I growl through my teeth.

He laughs wickedly as he inches closer. "I'll never stay away. Don't you get it? You're mine." Grabbing my waist, he pulls me close to him. I try to escape his clutch, but it's impossible. "You were mine from the first time I saw you at GPAC."

For the first time, all eyes fall on us. Dylan is about to be famous, but not in a good way.

"Like hell I was!" I say as a lean back from him.

"You are so full of shit, Charley! You know you wanted me, everyone does, but I made sure of it! That state championship made you fall hard. You were different, like a new event at a meet that I was going to win, and then I sealed the deal at Trent's. You fell for it so easily. I slipped that "Z" in your beer without you knowing. You were so naïve and stupid! Going to the bathroom was just classic!"

People begin to whisper and point, as we are on full display now. Something inside me snaps. I push him back, but he comes at me again. This time I can't push him off me, and I struggle to stand my ground. I use every ounce of force, but as soon as I'm ready to push away again, a fist comes in contact with his jaw. Cash.

Punch after punch, blow after blow, Cash continues to take out the past eighteen months of bottled-up emotions on him. Cash continues to hit him over and over. The sounds coming from Dylan's body are like none I have ever heard. There are cracks, crunches, whimpers, and howls. By the time Cash is finished, Dylan is lying in a fetal position in the dirt, not moving.

"You listen to me, motherfucker. Char-coal's not yours. She's mine."

To be continued... *Loving Charley* will release spring 2014

About the Author

Casey Peeler grew up and still lives in North Carolina with her husband and daughter. Her first passion is teaching students with special needs. Over the years, she found her way to relax was in a good book.

After reading *Their Eyes Were Watching God* by Zora Neal Hurston her senior year of high school and multiple Nicholas Sparks' novels, she found a hidden love and appreciation for reading.

Casey is an avid reader, blogger (Hardcover Therapy,) and now author. *No Turning Back* (Full Circle #1) is her debut novel released September 30th.

Her goal is to one day be an author who is recognized nationwide like Jamie McGuire, Colleen Hoover, Tiffany King, and Amanda Bennett.

When Casey isn't reading, you can find her listening to country music, spending the day at the lake, being a wife and dance mom, and spending time with friends and family.

Her perfect day consists of water, sand between her toes, a cold beverage, and a great book!

Website: http://authorcaseypeeler.weebly.com/
Facebook: www.facebook.com/caseypeelerauthor
Facebook Author Group: https://www.facebook.com/groups/219865574845739/
Twitter: www.twitter.com/AuthorCasey
Goodreads: http://www.goodreads.com/author/show/7106874.Casey_Peeler
Pinterest: http://www.pinterest.com/authorcasey/

http://www.pinterest.com/authorcasey/no-turning-back-full-circle-1/
http://www.pinterest.com/authorcasey/finding-charley-full-circle-2/
YouTube: https://www.youtube.com/channel/UC0lmpt4hErNau1woOOsJOnw

Add No Turning Back (Full Circle #1) to your TRB on Goodreads: www.goodreads.com/user/show/16117017-casey-peeler

Add Finding Charley (Full Circle #2) to your TBR on Goodreads: www.goodreads.com/book/show/18596891-finding-charley

9-14

DISCARD

CPSIA information can be obtained at www.ICGtesting.com
Printed in the USA
LVOW07s1520090914

403215LV00002B/420/P